FATALISM

Screenplay

by

THREE

DOGS

PRODUCTIONS

MARCELLO INTRALIGI

FRANCESCO GIAMPIETRO

WAYNE SHEPHERD

FATALISM

FADE IN:

1 - <u>INT. AN UNDERGROUND CAVERN - DUSK</u>

Total blackness. Suddenly--an agonized whisper:

FATHER TIMOTHY (V.O.)

Te ette voi tehdä tätä...minulle...[1] I am...a man of...<u>God</u>...

A CAPTION appears against the blackness: **NORTHERN EUROPE ~ AD 1005.**

Light flickers, illuminating a <u>CLOSE-SHOT</u> of 70-YEAR-OLD FATHER TIMOTHY's FACE, bruised and bloodied.

FATHER TIMOTHY

You...cannot...do this...to me...

FATHER TIMOTHY is chained to the cavern wall. Affixed to the wall on either side of him is a large <u>upside-down</u> crucifix. More than six-feet tall, dressed in black, face mostly hidden, a FIGURE stands in front of the priest.

CAPTOR

I can do whatever I <u>want</u> to you--priest! I <u>own</u> you now! <u>ANSWER ME</u>!

With one massive hand, he grips the priest's throat.

CAPTOR

<u>ANSWER ME</u>!

The priest's captor is <u>THE WARLORD AHRMAN</u>. In <u>CLOSE-UP</u>, we see his yellowed teeth, his sparse hair. <u>The rotting flesh of his face</u>.

---

[1] Finnish dialogue. Translation: "You cannot do this...to me..." Sub-title NOT needed.

1

FATHER TIMOTHY

(choking)

I...cannot answer...what I do not... know...

AHRMAN

Sinä VALEHTELET![2]

FATHER TIMOTHY

I...canno--

AHRMAN

YOU ARE LYING!!

AHRMAN's hand is squeezing the priest's throat harder and harder.

FATHER TIMOTHY

(pleading)

...kill...me...

With a bellow of frustration, AHRMAN whirls away from the priest--and magically disappears. FATHER TIMOTHY gasps for air. Then suddenly--

AHRMAN (O.S.)

(almost incoherent in his rage)

'Til dawn--priest. 'Til dawn!!

At FATHER TIMOTHY's feet are THREE CRYSTAL TABLETS arranged on a velvet cloth. Each is triangular, covered with ancient inscriptions.

---

[2] Finnish dialogue. Translation: "You are LYING!" Sub-title NOT needed.

AHRMAN (O.S.)

You have 'til dawn tomorrow--<u>priest</u>--to tell me the secret of these artifacts. To tell me what power it is that they hold. To tell me where the fourth piece can be found.

(pause)

If you do not...If you do not... I promise you...it will take me an entire <u>day</u> to end your miserable life...

FATHER TIMOTHY

DearGodinHeavenDearGodinHeav--

AHRMAN (O.S.)

And do not think that a night of prayer will help you--Father Timothy, your <u>holiness</u>. YOUR LIFE IS <u>MINE</u> NOW!

Suddenly, FATHER TIMOTHY screams in agony: two strips of flesh--one horizontal, one vertical--are magically peeling away from his bare torso. Once peeled, they form <u>a bloody upside-down cross</u>...

DISSOLVE TO:

2 - <u>EXT. MOUTH OF CAVERN - DUSK</u>

FATHER TIMOTHY's SCREAMS drift faintly to the mouth of the cave. Two YOUNG BOYS, clothed in hooded monk robes, creep stealthily into the opening. Their eyes are round with fear.

SHORTER BOY

That's Father Timothy that's Father Timothy that's Father Timoth--

TALLER BOY

(whispering)

Quiet! We'll find him. We'll save him. Just keep your mouth shut and follow me!

They move cautiously along the tunnel that leads from the cave opening. Without warning, something thrusts outwards from the tunnel wall--it's a HAND composed of rock! It seizes the SHORTER BOY by the throat, lifts him up. The TALLER BOY is unaware of what's going on behind him and keeps walking--that is, until he hears his friend choking...

TALLER BOY

(turning)
SHHH!!! I said keep your m--

The TALLER BOY sees what's happening: There are two ROCK HANDS now, gripping the SHORTER BOY's neck. His feet are kicking, inches above the ground. Before the TALLER BOY can rush to help, he witnesses the HANDS snap his friend's neck, then release the lifeless body to collapse to the ground. The TALLER BOY is stunned, even more so when another ROCK HAND punches outwards from the tunnel wall right in front of him. He ducks and dodges, sobbing as he runs for the cave entrance. With shocking speed, other ROCK HANDS are now thrusting out of the walls on both sides of him, clutching, grasping. He barely manages to escape to safety...

DISSOLVE TO:

3 - <u>EXT. KING GALEN'S CASTLE - ESTABLISHING SHOT - DUSK</u>

<u>ANGLE UPWARDS</u> to a third-floor window. Silhouetted there are two figures, holding each other, kissing...

4 - <u>INT. PRINCESS KATRINE'S BEDCHAMBER - THAT MOMENT</u>

KATRINE and ALEXANDER are kissing: KATRINE is the beautiful 20-year-old daughter of KING GALEN; ALEXANDER is a handsome 21-year-old prince. Without breaking their embrace, they move across the room. ALEXANDER's feet get tangled up with a quiver full of arrows and a bow lying on the floor. He and KATRINE both fall to the bed.

ALEXANDER

(kissing her)

Mihin minä kompastuin...tällä kertaa?[3]

KATRINE

(kissing him)

My bow and arrows... Sorry...

ALEXANDER

(kissing her)

I must be mad...to love someone as... untidy...as messy...as youmphh--

KATRINE shuts him up with her lips... <u>CLOSE-UP</u> ON KATRINE's LEFT HAND stroking ALEXANDER's hair: on the back of her hand is <u>a small birth-mark in the shape of the spread wingspan of a bird in flight.</u> Suddenly, there is URGENT HAMMERING at the door.

KATRINE

Minun isäni--?[4]

ALEXANDER

If it <u>is</u> your father, I'm a dead man--

KATRINE gives ALEXANDER a powerful shove--

ALEXANDER

Wha--?!

---

[3] Finnish dialogue. Translation: "What did I trip over...<u>this</u> time?" Sub-title NOT needed.
[4] Finnish dialogue. Translation: "My father--?" Sub-title NOT needed.

--he rolls off the bed and hits the floor, out of view.

MARCUS (O.S.)

Princess Katrine! I'm trying to find Prince Alexander! Is he with you--?

ALEXANDER's head appears above the edge of the bed.

ALEXANDER

It's only Marcus--

MARCUS HAMMERS on the door again.

MARCUS (O.S.)

Princess! *Onko Alexander sinun luonasi?!*[5]

KATRINE

Umm--Just a minute--

As KATRINE straightens her clothes, ALEXANDER gets to his feet and goes to the door. He opens it, and his face lights up.

ALEXANDER

Marcus!

MARCUS, in his early-40s, is KING GALEN's brilliant alchemist and, next to KATRINE, ALEXANDER's closest friend in the world. RONIM, MARCUS's dog, is by his side. ALEXANDER embraces him, a hug made awkward by the CRYSTAL ORB worn on a leather strap around MARCUS's neck.

MARCUS

Alexander. I must speak with you.

----

[5] Finnish dialogue. Translation: "Is Alexander with you?!" Sub-title NOT needed.

MARCUS looks over ALEXANDER's shoulder at KATRINE, as she smoothes the bed.

MARCUS

(to Katrine)
My apologies for the intrusion.

ALEXANDER

(bending down to scratch Ronim's ears)
Hey, Ronim--Good to see you again, boy.

MARCUS

Alexander--please--you must come with me--now--

ALEXANDER

But I can't. Not now. I was just about to...

ALEXANDER glances back over his shoulder. KATRINE is still straightening the bed. His eyes are shining as he removes something from his belt-pouch--we don't see what--and shows it to MARCUS.

ALEXANDER

(voice lowered)
I've been planning this for months.

MARCUS

I'm sorry. But that will have to wait--

KATRINE

(approaching them)
What will?

ALEXANDER shoves the object back into the pouch. KATRINE eyes him curiously.

MARCUS

Look--as much as I would love to stand here and chat--<u>there is no time</u>.

KATRINE and ALEXANDER stare at their friend.

MARCUS (CONT'D)

Something terrible has happened--

5 - <u>EXT. CASTLE STABLES - ESTABLISHING SHOT - NIGHT</u>

The castle stables are dark and deserted. Silent--

6 - <u>INT. CASTLE STABLES - THAT MOMENT</u>

KATRINE

What?!

MARCUS

<u>Quiet</u>. No one must hear us.

KATRINE and ALEXANDER are standing at the entrance to a stall, watching as MARCUS hastily saddles his horse. RONIM, his dog, is seated close by.

MARCUS (CONT'D)

I said: The Warlord Ahrman has abducted Father Timothy.

ALEXANDER

But--But--Why? <u>How</u>? My God--<u>Ahrman</u>?! Does King Galen know of this?

MARCUS

No. And we mustn't tell him. If he sends his soldiers to rescue Father Timothy... Ahrman will see them coming from miles away...and all hell will break loose...

KATRINE

But how do <u>you</u> know about this?

MARCUS

Two young boys from the monastery witnessed the abduction and followed them.
One of the children was murdered... By Ahrman.
 (angry pause)
We have until dawn to rescue Timothy.

ALEXANDER

But what does Ahrman hope to gain--?

MARCUS

I'll explain on the way. We must hurry.

KATRINE

But--what's your plan?

MARCUS holds up a hand--"just a moment"-- and hurries to the stone wall at the end of his horse's stall. He tugs out one of the stones, revealing a roomy cavity. He removes the CRYSTAL ORB from around his neck and places it in the hole.

KATRINE

Why are you leaving the orb behind? If you ever needed its protection, surely you need it tonight--

MARCUS

<u>No</u>. The orb stays here.

He pushes the stone firmly back in place.

DISSOLVE TO:

7 - <u>EXT. FOREST - NIGHT</u>

<u>*ANGLE ON*</u> *the half-hidden exit of a secret tunnel set into the hillside. MARCUS and KATRINE are on horseback beside the exit, waiting for ALEXANDER. At last, he rides out. There is something different about his appearance: his long hair is wet and slicked back. KATRINE stares at him curiously.*

                    KATRINE
Where did you get to? And why are you all wet--?

                    ALEXANDER
There was something I had to do.
(pause)
Look--Katrine--will you please--<u>please</u>... go back to the castle--?

                    KATRINE
Would you just <u>stop</u>--?! Either we both go with Marcus or neither of us goes.

KATRINE swings her horse, FIREBRAND, around to join MARCUS, who is just setting off. ALEXANDER follows, his face dark as a thundercloud.

8 - <u>EXT. FOREST (FURTHER IN) - NIGHT</u>

<u>*MOVING SHOT*</u>*: The TRIO rides through the moonlit forest.*

                    KATRINE
What's so important about these crystal tablets?

                    MARCUS
They are ancient...thousands of years old ...sacred beyond your imagining...

                    KATRINE
You've seen them?

MARCUS

My family was given the great privilege, many, many generations ago, of looking after the tablets. We were entrusted with them...to keep them safe.
(bitterly)
They were stolen from my grandfather when I was a boy...by petty thieves who had no idea what blasphemy they were perpetrating.

KATRINE

So how has Ahrman come into possession of them now?

MARCUS

I have no idea. Through some underhand dealing or other--who knows?
(pause)
<u>Immortality</u>. That's what he's after. That's what he's been obsessed with all his misbegotten life. He must believe that the tablets will somehow enable him to learn <u>the secret of living forever</u>.

KATRINE

And will they? Is that why he's abducted Father Timothy?

MARCUS

I don't know. All I'm sure of is that those three holy fragments of crystal... they are the key to an immense power...an unbelievable power...
(pause)
If Ahrman were ever to learn how to use that key...

There is a shadow of deepest dread in MARCUS's eyes.

DISSOLVE TO:

9 - <u>**EXT. EDGE OF FOREST - NIGHT**</u>

Hidden in the underbrush, ALEXANDER is peering out at the entrance to the cave where FATHER TIMOTHY is being held.

ALEXANDER

(low voice)

There are no guards!?

MARCUS

We can only pray that Ahrman has returned to his castle 'til dawn. He's a warlock, but he's still human. He must need to replenish his strength <u>sometimes</u>.

(pause)

But we must not forget the fate suffered by the child from the monastery. Move with great caution.

ALEXANDER starts to follow MARCUS--but KATRINE holds him back. She embraces him fiercely and kisses him on the lips.

KATRINE

We'll both be very careful. All right?

From ALEXANDER's expression, it's clear he doesn't think being careful will be enough.

10 - <u>INT. CAVERN ENTRANCE - NIGHT</u>

KATRINE, ALEXANDER and MARCUS draw their swords and enter the cave cautiously. They see the little boy's lifeless body on the ground and KATRINE drops to one knee at his side. She touches his face with great tenderness, then closes his staring eyes.

Suddenly, a ROCK HAND explodes from the tunnel wall. KATRINE dives out of its reach as it blindly gropes at the air to find her. ALEXANDER is there in an instant. With one mighty swing of his sword, he severs the ROCK HAND from the wall. It crumbles to bits.

MARCUS

LOOK OUT--!!!

Behind ALEXANDER, more than just a hand is forcing its way out of the wall: it's an entire body, a massive *HUMAN FIGURE* made of living stone, with black, empty eyes. ALEXANDER is caught off-guard. The *STONE CREATURE* seizes him by the throat. MARCUS hacks and hacks at the CREATURE with his sword--but to no avail. It seems that once the CREATURE has fully formed, a sword no longer has any effect on it. ALEXANDER drops his sword, choking. He struggles uselessly against the powerful rocky hands.

KATRINE

Marcus! Move!

KATRINE is already pulling her bow from her back, slapping an arrow into position. MARCUS sees what she's doing, steps aside. ALEXANDER's face is turning purple, his feet off the ground.

KATRINE lets the arrow fly. It hits the CREATURE--dead center in one of its black eyes. The CREATURE freezes. Then its hands snap open, releasing ALEXANDER. He stumbles away, gasping in air, as the CREATURE shudders and crumbles to pieces on the ground.

CUT TO:

11 - <u>INT. ANOTHER CAVERN - THAT MOMENT</u>

AHRMAN is "sleeping": in a sitting position, cross-legged, eyes closed--<u>levitating two feet off the ground</u>. Tendrils of crackling energy surround him, spiraling towards his body, as if <u>feeding him</u>, <u>recharging him</u>.

--<u>CLOSE-UP</u> on AHRMAN's decaying face--<u>as his eyes snap open</u>--

12 - <u>INT. FIRST CAVERN - THAT MOMENT</u>

ALEXANDER

Bastard. <u>Bastard</u>!

ALEXANDER, MARCUS and KATRINE are at the far side of the cavern, standing in front of FATHER TIMOTHY, still manacled to the rock wall. They are staring grimly at the bloody upside-down cross peeled into his bare torso. The old priest can no longer meet AHRMAN's dawn deadline: he has died as a result of his horrific injuries. MARCUS, with tears in his eyes, makes a quick sign-of-the-cross. Quickly, carefully, he then gathers the THREE CRYSTAL TABLETS and places them inside his satchel.

MARCUS

Come on--let's <u>go</u>!

13 - <u>EXT. EDGE OF KING GALEN'S FOREST - DAWN</u>

Out of the forest ride ALEXANDER, KATRINE and MARCUS. In front of them, across a clearing, is KING GALEN's castle: home, safety.

KATRINE

We made it! We weren't follo--

Suddenly, from <u>OFF SCREEN</u>: the approaching SOUND OF THUNDERING HOOVES. All heads turn as one. Across the clearing comes the WARLORD AHRMAN with an army of MUTANT SOLDIERS--massive, muscular, heavily-armored. Through their iron masks, we can see their misshapen faces and inhuman blood-red eyes.

ALEXANDER

<u>Jesus Christ Almighty</u>...

KATRINE

Is that--?

MARCUS

Yes. He's trying to cut us off.

ALEXANDER

(spurring his horse)
MOVE!!!

The three friends set off at a gallop across the clearing--as AHRMAN gets closer, closer...

14 - <u>EXT. CASTLE COURTYARD - DAWN</u>

TWO SENTRIES are hastily opening the gates. The battlements are full of CASTLE DWELLERS watching the chase in horror. KING GALEN is one of these onlookers. His eyes widen.

KING GALEN

Prepare for battle! It is <u>Ahrman</u>!

The courtyard is thronging with activity: SOLDIERS everywhere, readying their weapons.

ALEXANDER, MARCUS and KATRINE gallop through the open gateway. Behind them-- so close!--are AHRMAN and his army. The gates are closed with only seconds to spare. AHRMAN's leading riders collide thunderously with the just-shut barrier.

<u>And then there is ABSOLUTE SILENCE</u>. Suddenly, no sounds of horses, no voices- -nothing. Within the courtyard, it's as though everyone is holding their breath, waiting.

The VIEW OVER THE BATTLEMENTS reveals the reason for the silence: AHRMAN and his army have disappeared!

SOLDIER

Sire, they're gone--vanished!

All at once, there is a HUGE EXPLOSION. In the courtyard, dirt erupts up into the air, in one, two, ten, thirty places. Clods of earth shoot up like geysers. Thick clouds of dust billow. CASTLE DWELLERS and SOLDIERS are sent flying. And amidst all this confusion, we see
<u>*AHRMAN and his SOLDIERS magically rising up out of the ground.*</u>

Panic! Screams! The clash of swords! Blood! People running. KING GALEN's SOLDIERS fighting bravely, but with little hope of winning...

AHRMAN

You cannot win this battle! <u>Return my tablets to me!</u>

KATRINE

<u>Go to hell!</u>

AHRMAN, still on horseback, turns to face KATRINE. KATRINE, also still on horseback, has her bow raised, an arrow aimed directly at AHRMAN. His decaying face repulses her. KATRINE lets the arrow fly. It hits AHRMAN in the throat. He doesn't flinch or cry out. But his eyes blaze with fury.

At that instant, AHRMAN's SOLDIERS grip their own throats in agony, as if <u>they</u> are experiencing AHRMAN's wound. KING GALEN's SOLDIERS take swift advantage of their pain and distraction. They attack AHRMAN's army with renewed determination. Amazingly, the instant AHRMAN'S SOLDIERS are pierced with swords, their bodies decompose and crumble to dust. Suits of armor clatter to the ground, empty.

<u>*CLOSE-UP*</u> *on AHRMAN's neck:* <u>*with a magical CRACKLING SOUND, the arrow is pushing itself out of his skin.*</u> *But even as the wound speed-heals, new patches of rot*

appear on his face. Clearly, there is a price to pay for all the magical energy he's been expending.

AHRMAN

Little...<u>bitch</u>--

On the word "bitch," AHRMAN <u>hurls</u> a blast of

MARCUS

KATRINE--<u>MOVE</u>--!!

Supernatural energy at KATRINE and her horse, FIREBRAND. It envelops them-- and instantly <u>they begin to rise up off the ground</u>. ALEXANDER rushes at AHRMAN; but the WARLORD clubs him aside. ALEXANDER falls to the ground, conscious, but dazed.

KATRINE and FIREBRAND are now <u>twenty-five feet in the air</u>, and still rising. Desperate, KATRINE unrolls a coil of rope that is attached to her saddle. Quickly, she ties the rope to one of her stirrups.

MARCUS

Katrine--!

KATRINE and FIREBRAND stop rising at about sixty feet. The rope is secured to the stirrup.

KING GALEN

HURRY! <u>HURRY</u>!

KATRINE begins to <u>climb down</u> FIREBRAND's side, holding on to the harness for dear life. KING GALEN, ALEXANDER and MARCUS look up in horror. RONIM barks furiously. AHRMAN stares up, grinning; his hands are at his sides, his fists clenched. KATRINE is holding on to the stirrup now. FIREBRAND's legs are *uselessly beating the air. KATRINE rests the palm of her free hand for a moment against FIREBRAND's side.*

KATRINE

Oh God, Firebrand--<u>please forgive me</u>--

And she begins to climb as fast as she can, down the dangling rope. Within seconds, the climb turns into a frantic slide and her hands burn and smoke.

ALEXANDER & KING GALEN

(simultaneously)

<u>KATRINE</u>!

AHRMAN's EYES are glazed as if he's in some kind of sadistic trance.

Unable to hold on any longer, <u>KATRINE releases the rope</u>. She falls the rest of the way and hits the ground mere inches from a wooden fence with pointed pickets. She rolls on impact, until her body comes up hard against a stone wall. Her head hits it with a brutal CRACK. She lies pale, deathly still.

<u>A TIGHT SHOT</u> of AHRMAN'S HANDS: all at once, his fists open--

The aura around FIREBRAND <u>vanishes</u>--and she plummets to her death.

KING GALEN charges like a madman at AHRMAN and plunges his sword into the WARLORD's back. AHRMAN falls to the ground. ALEXANDER is kneeling beside KATRINE attempting, unsuccessfully to wake her. His eyes are bright with tears.

Suddenly, RONIM the dog lunges at AHRMAN, sinking his teeth into his hand. We see AHRMAN's ROTTING FACE--he cannot lift his head, he's dying. Even so, his eyes narrow...<u>and blaze with green fire</u>...

KING GALEN

(looking down on AHRMAN)
Devil...! <u>DEVIL</u>--!

The green fire disappears from AHRMAN's eyes, leaving them empty and dead. There is a crackle of green energy at the point of contact between RONIM's teeth and AHRMAN's hand. Then this fizzles out--and <u>the fire returns to AHRMAN's eyes</u> where it flickers weakly. KING GALEN raises his sword, two-handed.

KING GALEN

God damn you to <u>HELL</u>--!

Near death, panic-stricken, AHRMAN tries again, grimacing with effort: the green fire vanishes from his eyes, reappears where RONIM's teeth have seized his hand--as KING GALEN swings his sword powerfully down--and this time the crackling green energy reappears <u>in RONIM's eyes</u>. <u>AHRMAN has succeeded in passing his life-force into RONIM's body</u>--at the exact instant that KING GALEN's sword cuts off AHRMAN's head!

ALEXANDER is cradling KATRINE's unmoving body in his arms, tears streaming down his cheeks. KING GALEN and MARCUS kneel beside them. And RONIM nuzzles MARCUS's hand with completely realistic affection.

DISSOLVE TO:

15 - <u>EXT. DECK OF *BIRD OF PARADISE* - DAY</u>

Some months have passed. ALEXANDER sits, brooding, near the SHIP'S PROW. He is bearded, his hair longer, wilder, his solemn face tanned. A hand comes INTO FRAME and rests on his shoulder.

MARCUS

It _will_ work. You _must_ have faith.

ALEXANDER says nothing. MARCUS, bearded and tanned too, sits down beside him.

MARCUS

You _must_ believe in the tablets. The secrets they've revealed to us. There is so much _more_ to this now than simply rousing Katrine from her...from her perpetual sleep... We cannot even _begin_ to comprehend the full implications.

ALEXANDER

But what if we're _wrong_? What if we misinterpreted the symbols? What if we're out here on this Godforsaken voyage _and we're WRONG_?

MARCUS

We are _not_ wrong. We are doing what we must. God has _not_ forsaken us.

The Bird of Paradise _plows onward towards the horizon._

16 - <u>INT. CABIN (BELOW DECK) - EVENING</u>

On a long oak table sits a casket made of gray stone, its sides carved with intricate ornamentation. The casket lid is leaning against the wall. ALEXANDER is gazing down into the casket, his eyes shining.

ALEXANDER

<u>Please</u>. Please wake up...

KATRINE is lying inside the casket, her eyes closed, her face white. ALEXANDER takes her limp hand and presses it desperately against his lips. We see again the strange birthmark on the back of her hand...

17 - <u>EXT. DECK OF _BIRD OF PARADISE_ - DAY</u>

The sails of the ship hang limp. ALEXANDER and MARCUS, on deck with some CREW-MEN, are looking up, troubled.

ALEXANDER

How much longer--?

The ship's CAPTAIN approaches. He looks upset, confused.

CAPTAIN

I'm sorry, my lords--I have...I have more bad news...

MARCUS

What?

CAPTAIN

I...I'm afraid, my lords, that we are... lost...

ALEXANDER

Lost?!

MARCUS

What do you mean?! How can we be lost--?!

CAPTAIN

I...do not know, my lord. It seems that... It appears that all our navigational devices have been directing us falsely for...for at least--I would guess-- three days--

ALEXANDER

But that's impossible--!

CAPTAIN

Well...it's either the navigational devices...or...

(pause)

...or every single star, planet...the moon--even the sun...every single heavenly body has shifted positions in the sky...

RONIM comes up beside MARCUS and licks his hand. For a fleeting moment, a malignant green light radiates from the DOG's EYES...

18 - EXT. DECK OF *BIRD OF PARADISE* - NIGHT

The ship's sails are still limp. Everything is frozen, waiting...

MARCUS (V.O.)

We have no choice--

19 - INT. KATRINE'S CABIN - THAT MOMENT

ALEXANDER is standing beside the open casket, his hand resting on KATRINE's arm. MARCUS paces restlessly.

ALEXANDER

If we don't get back on course soon...she might...she might die...

MARCUS nods, thinking.

MARCUS

We must take the next step, go to the next level...

ALEXANDER

You don't think...could there be any danger...?

MARCUS

I have absolutely no idea! No one knows the true power of the orb, what it's capable of. And bringing it together with the tablets...

(sighs)

We just have to pray that doing this will give us the guidance we need...will enable us to reach our destination in time...

At last, the momentous decision has been made.

MARCUS

Is the door locked?

ALEXANDER nods. MARCUS removes the THREE CRYSTAL TABLETS from his satchel and lays them on the table. Suddenly, the CRYSTAL ORB that hangs around MARCUS's neck begins to glow. The TABLETS flash and gleam. ALEXANDER and MARCUS stare in awe.

ALEXANDER

Look!

All at once, THREE SLOTS appear on the ORB's previously smooth exterior. At the same moment, from beyond the locked cabin door, we hear a DOG's FRANTIC WHINE, then URGENT SCRATCHING.

MARCUS

You'd better let him in. We need absolute silence.

ALEXANDER unlocks and opens the door--to the accompaniment of an ANGRY RUMBLE OF THUNDER from outside. RONIM enters, running directly to MARCUS. ALEXANDER relocks the door. Suddenly, the ship lurches. ALEXANDER and MARCUS grab the table for support.

ALEXANDER

We need wind, not a storm...

MARCUS detaches the ORB from its leather strap and hands it to ALEXANDER. The ORB's light spears between his fingers. RONIM watches intently. We notice, *behind the dog's left ear, a peeling patch of fur, the flesh <u>decaying</u>... THUNDER BOOMS again, and the SOUND OF HEAVY RAIN can now be heard. The ship is rocking uneasily.*

ALEXANDER

Should we check--?

MARCUS

<u>Shhh</u>!

ALEXANDER holds the ORB as MARCUS takes the first of the THREE TRIANGULAR TABLETS and inserts its point into one of the newly-formed slots on the sphere's surface. It CLICKS into place, causing the ORB's glow to <u>intensify</u>. The long-absent WIND has now returned from nowhere, in full force--

20 - <u>EXT. DECK OF *BIRD OF PARADISE* - THAT MOMENT</u>

The Bird of Paradise *is being tossed about, waves crashing against its hull. Deck-hands scurry in panic.*

21 - <u>INT. KATRINE'S CABIN - THAT MOMENT</u>

RONIM watches eagerly as MARCUS clicks the SECOND and THIRD TABLETS into the ORB. The ORB, its glow now almost blinding, begins to <u>vibrate</u> in ALEXANDER's hands. Startled, he almost drops it--

MARCUS

Don't worry. <u>Let go of it</u>.

ALEXANDER stares at him.

MARCUS

Let <u>go</u> of it.

The ORB, with the INSERTED TABLETS, <u>floats</u> when ALEXANDER releases it. ALEXANDER, MARCUS and even RONIM squint against the brilliant luminescence. In the casket, KATRINE is bathed in the holy light. All at once, the ORB starts to <u>rotate</u>, slowly at first, then faster, and faster--and the brilliant light pulses, on and off, on and off--

--SUDDENLY!--although MARCUS, ALEXANDER, RONIM--AND KATRINE IN THE CASKET-- remain IN FOCUS, everything else <u>starts to change</u>: Background objects lose their sharpness, become blurry, hazy, colors shifting, smudging. The entire ship's cabin seems to be <u>physically transforming</u> around them--

--but before the transformation is complete, <u>LIGHTNING STRIKES</u>--

22 - <u>EXT. DECK OF *BIRD OF PARADISE* - THAT MOMENT</u>

The tallest mast has been struck by lightning. It cracks, splits, then comes slowly CRASHING down. It SMASHES through the deck--

23 - <u>INT. KATRINE'S CABIN - THAT MOMENT</u>

--the flaming mast SMASHES through the ceiling of KATRINE's cabin, sending MARCUS, ALEXANDER and RONIM sprawling to the floor. At that instant, the FLOATING ORB's light fades and <u>each of the THREE TABLETS slides simultaneously out of its slot</u>--

MARCUS

(struggling to his feet)
The orb--!!

ALEXANDER dives across the cabin and catches the falling ORB; the TABLETS, however, hit the floor and slide away. Amidst the flames, smoke and rain that now fill the cabin, MARCUS retrieves them.

ALEXANDER

We're trapped!

The burning mast is wedged up against the cabin door.

MARCUS

Where's Ronim?!

Just then, a RAGGED SHOUT is HEARD from overhead:

CAPTAIN

Lord Marcus! Up here!

The CAPTAIN, lying on the deck above, reaches down into the hole smashed in the cabin's ceiling.

CAPTAIN

Take my hand! I can pull you both up!

MARCUS

No! First take the tablets! Get them to safety!

MARCUS climbs onto the table bearing KATRINE'S casket. <u>But he cannot reach the CAPTAIN's hand</u>.

ALEXANDER

The lid!

MARCUS jumps down, and he and ALEXANDER heave up the casket lid. They lay it on top of the casket, at just enough of an angle that KATRINE's face and torso are still uncovered. MARCUS climbs back onto the table, then onto the casket lid. Now he is able to reach the CAPTAIN's hand. MARCUS passes him first ONE TABLET, then the SECOND, and the CAPTAIN tucks them safely into his shirt.

MARCUS

One more!

(looks down at Alexander)

Give me the orb, too!

ALEXANDER hands MARCUS the ORB. But before MARCUS can pass it or the THIRD TABLET up to the CAPTAIN, there is a BOOMING CRASH as a colossal wave explodes against the ship's hull. The CAPTAIN is swept away--<u>along with two of the precious TABLETS</u>...

24 - <u>EXT. DECK OF *BIRD OF PARADISE* - THAT MOMENT</u>

SCREAMING CREW-MEN jump from the burning deck. The ship is being tossed, spun, buffeted, and battered.

25 - <u>INT. KATRINE'S CABIN - THAT MOMENT</u>

Water rushes in through the hull, swirling around MARCUS and ALEXANDER, who were both knocked to the floor when the last wave hit.

MARCUS

We've got to close the casket!

ALEXANDER

<u>What</u>?!

MARCUS struggles through the rising water over to ALEXANDER, reattaching the CRYSTAL ORB to its leather strap. He pushes the ORB and the THIRD TABLET into ALEXANDER's hands.

MARCUS

Loop the orb around Katrine's neck! And put the tablet in the casket with her!

ALEXANDER stares at his friend in blank, horrified confusion.

                              MARCUS

DO IT!

ALEXANDER sloshes over to KATRINE's casket. He lifts KATRINE's head and loops the leather strap around her neck. He places the ORB on her breast. He tucks the THIRD TABLET under her arm. <u>Suddenly, the ORB starts to glow</u>.

                            ALEXANDER

<u>Why are we doing this</u>?!

                              MARCUS

We're...going down! It's her only chance! With the orb protecting her--

                            ALEXANDER

<u>But we can't</u>--!

                              MARCUS

We <u>must</u>!

They stare at each other. ALEXANDER's eyes are begging for another way.

                              MARCUS

We have to hurry! Help me with the--

                            ALEXANDER

Wait!

ALEXANDER leans over KATRINE's peaceful face. He grips her arm.

                            ALEXANDER

Katrine...I--I love you... I will... always... Oh God... Oh God...

He cannot finish. Desperately, he presses his lips against hers. He can't break the kiss, <u>won't</u> break the kiss, because he <u>knows</u>--

MARCUS
(touches Alexander's arm)
Alexander...

At last, ALEXANDER lets go of KATRINE's arm. The water is waist-high now. ALEXANDER and MARCUS pull the casket lid straight. The instant the stone lid slides into place, a multi-colored crystal growth begins to form: within seconds, it envelops the entire casket, cocoon-like. Suddenly, the cabin tilts violently to one side. Water explodes in through the disintegrating hull, engulfing <u>everything</u>--

26 - <u>EXT. DECK OF *BIRD OF PARADISE* - THAT MOMENT</u>

The great ship sinks slowly into the sea...

27 - <u>INT. KATRINE'S CABIN - NIGHT</u>

Furniture floats inside the fully submerged cabin. TWO DEAD BODIES float as well: MARCUS and ALEXANDER. KATRINE's CASKET tumbles slowly out through a gaping hole in the hull of the doomed ship...

28 - <u>EXT. THE SEA - THAT MOMENT</u>

KATRINE's CASKET drifts down...down...through the dark water...down ...down...until, finally, it comes to rest at the bottom of the sea...sending up clouds of sand...and <u>a swirling stream of BUBBLES</u>--

<u>MOVING SHOT ON</u> THE BUBBLES as they slowly rise through the dark water...through the dark water that is gradually becoming <u>lighter</u>, calmer--and the BUBBLES rise, rise to the water's surface before--

29 - <u>EXT. SURFACE OF THE SEA - MORNING</u>

--bursting into the open air is a DEEP-SEA DIVER. His suit and equipment are definitely <u>not</u> of the 11th century. Beyond the DIVER is a sleek white VESSEL with the name AVIANA painted on its hull. Below, in smaller lettering, are the words: BIANCHI MARINE ARCHEOLOGY EXPLORATIONS. The DIVER faces the CREW-MEMBERS gathered on the deck.

DIVER

(through diving-helmet)

I found something!

He begins to swim towards the ship, and as he does.

FADE OUT

<u>AGAINST THE BLACKNESS</u>, we HEAR distant MACHINERY, CHAINS CLANKING. Nearer, there is a CLICK--and then a <u>CIRCULAR VIEW</u> appears on the black screen, like a <u>telescope lens</u>. <u>FROM A HIGH VANTAGE POINT</u>, we are looking down at:

30 - <u>EXT. DECK OF *AVIANA* - AFTERNOON</u>

CREW-MEMBERS gather around a powerful WINCH. THE CIRCULAR VIEW-FRAME passes over the HORIZONTAL ARM OF A CRANE stretched out over the water, then down the THICK LINKS OF THE CHAIN that is lowering a LARGE RECTANGULAR CONTAINER into the sea. THE TELESCOPE CIRCLE SWINGS BACK TO THE DECK, to two FEMALE CREW-MEMBERS peering at a computer screen. One is wearing shorts and a low-cut tank-top. The telescope focuses on this YOUNG WOMAN's breasts, then <u>ZOOMS IN</u>. <u>CLICKS</u> are heard--for this telescope is also a CAMERA...

CREWMAN JOHNNY (O.S.)

Peter! That's uncharted territory you're spying on, lad! Very dangerous!

<u>THE TELESCOPE-CAMERA JERKS AWAY FROM</u> the YOUNG WOMAN's CHEST--

                          PETER (O.S.)

Shit...

We switch to a <u>*FULL SCREEN--PETER's BIRD'S-EYE POV DOWNWARDS*</u> *shows CREWMAN JOHNNY looking up with a big smile on his face.*

                            PETER

Oh--hey, Johnny...!

                      CREWMAN JOHNNY

You being a pervert again, are you, lad?

PETER THOMPSON, a good-looking 15-year-old with hair down to his shoulders, is perched in the crow's nest. He stuffs the INSTANT-PHOTOS he just took into his pocket and collapses his TELESCOPE-CAMERA.

                            PETER

I was just--uh--watching for Uncle Nick to come up again.

                      CREWMAN JOHNNY

I think the odds are a bit small, lad, that your Uncle Nicholas is going to resurface from the depths of Sharon's tank-top.
(pause)
Now--are you coming down to give us a hand, or what...?

PETER rolls his eyes and grudgingly starts to climb down.

31 - <u>EXT. DECK OF *AVIANA* - AFTERNOON</u>

CREW-MEMBERS assemble around a huge "ACCLIMATIZATION TANK." SHARON, the second-in-command, operates the attached computer console. Meanwhile, CREWMAN JOHNNY and PETER are leaning over the ship's rail, gazing down at the water.

PETER

What d'you think it is, Uncle Nick found? Maybe more artifacts like yesterday?

CREWMAN JOHNNY

Whatever it is, it's very large.
 (pause)
I wish he'd get a bloody move on. He's been down a long time.

There are sudden SHOUTS from the CREW; fingers point at the water.

CREWMAN JOHNNY

There they are!

THREE HELMETED DIVERS have just come to the surface. One of them--NICHOLAS BIANCHI, the diver we <u>first</u> saw--gives the "PULL UP" signal to SHARON. She pushes up a lever. The chain begins to rise out of the sea, eventually pulling up with it a large rectangular CONTAINER. CHEERS and WHISTLES erupt from the spectating CREW.

32 - <u>EXT. DECK OF AVIANA - AFTERNOON</u>

NICHOLAS BIANCHI is on deck now, facing the ACCLIMATIZATION TANK. We are looking at him FROM THE BACK as he supervises the CONTAINER being lowered <u>into</u> the TANK. The CONTAINER sinks slowly, jostles--

NICHOLAS

<u>Slowly</u>! Be <u>careful</u>!!

--then comes to rest at the bottom of the TANK. NICHOLAS presses a few buttons, and the CONTAINER opens inside the TANK. The DISCOVERED OBJECT is revealed: <u>KATRINE's CASKET</u> within its crystal cocoon!

ANGLE ON NICHOLAS BIANCHI: For the first time, we see his face. He is a handsome man of 28, lean, tanned. And one other thing: he is the spitting image of the long-dead PRINCE ALEXANDER...!

33 - <u>INT. *AVIANA* (BELOW DECK), NICHOLAS'S OFFICE - AFTERNOON</u>

NICHOLAS, SHARON and two CREW-MEMBERS are present. On NICHOLAS's desk are TWO FRAMED PHOTOGRAPHS: one of NICHOLAS and an ATTRACTIVE YOUNG WOMAN, both in wedding attire; the second of NICHOLAS, a younger PETER, and a DIFFERENT WOMAN--about 40 years old, attractive, a little overweight--on a beach at night, NICHOLAS playing the guitar, PETER and the WOMAN holding hands and singing.

NICHOLAS

We leave it in the tank for at least three hours.

SHARON

But why the extra time?

NICHOLAS

I want the acclimatizing process to be slowed down. Let the chemicals seep into the water at half-speed. I don't want that chest to be exposed to the air until it's been well and truly treated. Is that clear?

SHARON

(with a shrug)
You're the boss.

NICHOLAS

This discovery could finally make our reputation!

As he's talking, he rips a page from his desk-calendar, revealing today's date: April 23rd, 2005.

NICHOLAS (CONT'D)

I don't want anything to go wrong because we rushed the process.
(pause)
Besides...Pete and I need to take a launch back to the mainland for a couple of hours...

34 - <u>EXT. CHURCH CEMETERY - AFTERNOON</u>

A MARBLE HEADSTONE occupies the foreground; at some distance behind is a beautiful CHURCH; and beyond that, a picturesque view that tells us we're close to the COAST OF NAPLES, ITALY. The HEADSTONE reads:
PATRICIA BIANCHI, BELOVED WIFE OF NICHOLAS
JULY 5, 1978 – APRIL 23, 2002

Beside this is a SECOND HEADSTONE that reads:
JOANNA THOMPSON, DEVOTED MOTHER OF PETER
CHERISHED SISTER OF NICHOLAS
OCTOBER 8, 1962 – APRIL 23, 2002

Each HEADSTONE bears an inlaid photograph of the woman it commemorates--the two women from NICHOLAS's desk-photos. NICHOLAS and PETER are sitting close to one another, facing the HEADSTONES. Their eyes are glistening with tears. Suddenly--we are <u>INSIDE NICHOLAS's HEAD</u>: He and a younger PETER are on a motor-launch, approaching a vessel similar to the AVIANA. JOANNA and PATRICIA are waving to them from the deck, laughing. Without warning, there is a terrible explosion and the ship disappears in a horrific ball of flame...

Sitting on his mother's grave, PETER starts to sob. NICHOLAS circles his arm around his nephew's shoulders and holds him.

35 - <u>EXT. CHURCH - LATE AFTERNOON</u>

NICHOLAS and PETER are walking towards the church parking lot.

FATHER MICHAEL

Nicholas! Is that Nicholas Bianchi?!

NICHOLAS and PETER turn. FATHER MICHAEL is standing by the church where he's been scrubbing away graffiti; what's left is: **--CK THE CHURCH**. *Reluctantly, NICHOLAS and PETER approach. FATHER MICHAEL tosses his brush into a bucket on the steps beside him. Next to the bucket is a NEWSPAPER whose headline reads:* **TASK FORCE FORMED; SERIAL-KILLER ELUDES POLICE AS THIRD VICTIM BURIED**. *Below this, a COMPOSITE DRAWING of what the police believe to be the KILLER's FACE. At the top of the page, the date, April 22nd, 2005--yesterday.*

FATHER MICHAEL

(shaking Nicholas's and Peter's hands)
Nicholas, Peter--what a pleasant surprise.
(pause)
We don't see you at mass anymore, Nicholas. How have you been--?

NICHOLAS

I'm sure you can understand, Father, why we don't really have much desire to visit the House of the Lord anymore.

FATHER MICHAEL

I'm sorry you feel that way.
(pause)
God can help you get through this, you know. God can work wonders--

NICHOLAS

Pardon me, Father--and I really don't mean to be rude--but if there truly is a God, what has he <u>ever</u> done for Peter and me?

FATHER MICHAEL can't answer. The gold crucifix around his neck gleams weakly in the sunlight...

36 - <u>EXT. BIANCHI MARINE LABORATORY - ESTABLISHING SHOT - DUSK</u>

A modern-looking building situated close to the harbor...

37 - <u>INT. BIANCHI MARINE LABORATORY - DUSK</u>

NICHOLAS and PETER are standing at the head of KATRINE's CASKET, which is still enveloped by its crystal cocoon. At the other end are SHARON, CREWMAN JOHNNY, plus another CREWMAN (named ALDO). On the table on which the casket sits, we see hammers and chisels and littered fragments of crystal: the casket's 1000-year seal has been broken.

NICHOLAS

Let's do it.

NICHOLAS and PETER grip the head corners of the casket lid; SHARON and JOHNNY do the same at the foot. They manage to slide the lid a little. Abruptly, both NICHOLAS and PETER stop, leaving the lid resting across the lower half of the casket at an angle.

SHARON

What is it?

PETER

Holy...<u>crap</u>...

SHARON, JOHNNY and ALDO move to the head of the casket.

SHARON

Oh--!

PETER

It's a...a <u>statue</u>...?

In the casket lies KATRINE. She looks <u>exactly</u> as she did when we last saw her, one thousand years ago; <u>she hasn't aged a single day</u>. The ORB still rests on her breast, protecting her although it's no longer emanating light...

SHARON

It's so...<u>beautiful</u>...

NICHOLAS can't speak. He leans forward, hesitantly touches the ORB. There is <u>a momentary flicker of pale blue light</u> from within. No one notices because NICHOLAS's hand is in the way.

PETER

D'you think we should--?

The "STATUE" <u>MOANS</u>. Everyone literally jumps backwards. PETER stumbles and falls.

SHARON

What--?

PETER

(scrambling to his feet)
Whuh-What was <u>that</u>--?!

NICHOLAS

I...I don't think this is a statue...

<u>ANGLE ON</u> *KATRINE's FACE as she slowly begins to <u>awaken</u>...*

PETER

It's--she's--<u>alive</u>--?

NICHOLAS steps forward and takes hold of the lid again.

NICHOLAS

Help me.

Everyone helps. Slowly, the lid is moved. Suddenly, just as the lid is about to be lifted away, a DARK SHAPE hurls itself out of the casket. The casket-lid is almost dropped. The DARK SHAPE SLAMS into the wall--

PETER

--a <u>dog</u>--?!

The small DOG--RONIM!--is trembling, its teeth bared, its eyes darting wildly about the room. It sees a door slightly open. Before anyone can react, it rushes from the lab.

SHARON

What the hell...?

Another MOAN comes from inside the casket. KATRINE opens her eyes slowly, blinking, squinting.

KATRINE

Where...Where am I?

SHARON

She's <u>speaking</u>...

KATRINE

Where am I?

NICHOLAS can't speak. He is staring into the casket, stunned.

KATRINE

Please...where <u>am</u> I...?

NICHOLAS

That seal...was <u>hundreds</u> of years old...I analyzed it myself... This...this hasn't been opened for--for <u>hundreds of years</u>...

KATRINE lapses once more into unconsciousness.

38 - <u>EXT. HARBOR-FRONT WAREHOUSE COMPLEX - NIGHT</u>

The DOG hurries along the lane-ways between warehouses. It seems to be searching for something. Suddenly, it stops and its eyes glow with green fire. Then it sets off with renewed purpose...

39 - <u>EXT. HARBOR-FRONT WAREHOUSE COMPLEX - NIGHT</u>

The DOG pads along a pathway between two warehouses. We hear a WOMAN GASPING, MOANING. The DOG turns a corner--then <u>stops</u>--

FROM THE DOG's POV we see a tall, muscular MAN kissing a WOMAN, pressing her against a wall with his body. <u>He is also pressing the blade of a knife against the WOMAN's neck.</u>

<u>CLOSE-UP</u> of the WOMAN's FACE, her eyes wide with terror, as the MAN begins to press harder with the knife, slicing into her flesh--

Suddenly, the DOG <u>leaps</u> at the MAN. It clamps its jaws around his left ankle.

MAN

(spinning around)
What the fu--?!

The movement releases his hold on the WOMAN. She sinks to the ground, in shock. The DOG's eyes blaze with green fire as its jaws remain clamped to the MAN, no matter how much he tries to kick free. <u>AHRMAN is attempting to transfer his life-force from the body of the DOG into the MAN's</u>--but the required *effort is <u>immense</u>: this act of sorcery is becoming increasingly difficult for him to do. At last, though, it works--<u>and the green fire appears in the MAN's eyes</u>. AHRMAN has succeeded in transferring his life-force <u>into the body of this KILLER</u>!*

AHRMAN looks around at his unfamiliar surroundings. He kicks his ankle free from RONIM's now loosened jaws. The DOG runs off. AHRMAN sees the WOMAN. He kneels down beside her and places two fingers on her neck-wound. It heals instantly. He then covers her face with his hand. For a moment, she attempts to resist, but she isn't strong enough. Suddenly, a light emanates from her body--and then she starts to convulse. After a few moments, AHRMAN removes his hand from her face. The WOMAN opens her eyes and we see that they are now totally <u>red</u> in color. <u>AHRMAN has put her into some kind of possessed trance</u>...

40 - <u>INT. BIANCHI MARINE LABORATORY - NIGHT</u>

NICHOLAS, PETER, SHARON, JOHNNY and ALDO gaze down at KATRINE, still lying unconscious inside the casket. The ORB still rests on her breast. Suddenly, KATRINE stirs--

                              SHARON

Oh--!

KATRINE MOANS SOFTLY, twisting her head back and forth.

                              KATRINE

Firebrand... <u>Firebrand</u>...

She opens her eyes. Blinks blearily at SHARON, who is closest to her.

                              SHARON

H-Hello.

KATRINE tries to push herself up to a sitting position, but can't.

KATRINE

(groggily)
Who--Who are you? Where am I?

KATRINE's vision is blurry. SHARON leans closer, but KATRINE is only able to see some hazy facial features. The others in the group are even more indistinct.

SHARON

My name is Sharon--

KATRINE raises herself a little, shaking her head...

KATRINE

Where am I? Where is Alexander? My father?

KATRINE struggles to pull herself out of the casket. SHARON puts a hand on her arm.

SHARON

Please--don't panic. We're here to help you--

NICHOLAS moves closer to the head of the casket, and SHARON steps aside. KATRINE, her vision clearing, sees him. She gasps. Using all her strength, she half-climbs, half-falls out of the casket. NICHOLAS barely manages to catch her in his arms.

KATRINE

(hugging Nicholas tightly)
Thank God! Oh, thank God!

NICHOLAS holds on to KATRINE, not knowing what else to do.

KATRINE

What's happening?! Why does everything look so strange?! And who is this woman?

(holds him tighter)

Alexander--where is my father? And Marcus? Are the tablets safe?

NICHOLAS looks her in the eye, baffled.

KATRINE

What's wrong? Why won't you answer me?

(beat)

Is it my father?! Is he all right?

NICHOLAS

Please--you must calm down...

KATRINE draws back from NICHOLAS. She touches his hair, frowning.

KATRINE

Your hair... It's been cut off...

(pause)

Alexander--what is happening here?!

KATRINE looks at SHARON, at PETER, at JOHNNY and ALDO.

KATRINE

Did Ahrman do this? Is this some kind of-- magic spell?

(pause)

Tell me!

NICHOLAS leads KATRINE to a nearby chair, urges her to sit. He hunkers down in front of her, takes her hand.

NICHOLAS

(gently)

Can you tell me what your name is?

KATRINE stares at him. Then <u>explodes</u>:

KATRINE

What do you <u>mean</u>, tell you my name?! Have you lost your mind?!

NICHOLAS

<u>Please</u>--

KATRINE

Alexander, you're frightening me...!

SHARON

Why do you keep calling him "Alexander"? His name's Nicholas--

KATRINE

<u>What</u>?

NICHOLAS

I'm Nicholas Bianchi. This is Sharon Cox, my assistant. And my nephew, Peter--

PETER

You can call me Pete if you like--

KATRINE jumps to her feet. She stands facing everyone, trembling.

KATRINE

(to Nicholas)

Why are you doing this? I know you don't have a nephew!! What's happening?! Where have you brought me?!

NICHOLAS

Look, I'm sorry--I don't know who you think I--

KATRINE

Ahrman _is_ doing this! I know it! His sorcery is playing tricks with my mind!

NICHOLAS

Look, you _must_ calm down. Who is this... Ahrman, you keep talking about--?

Without warning, there is a thunderous CRASH as the lab door explodes inwards. AHRMAN, in his new form, stands in the doorway with ELSA, the woman he has entranced. In the resulting alarm and confusion, AHRMAN recognizes KATRINE.

AHRMAN

Little...<u>bitch</u>--

CLOSE-UP ON KATRINE: She's confused--she recognizes the voice but not the face--

KATRINE

Ahrman...?

NICHOLAS strides towards AHRMAN.

NICHOLAS

Just who the hell do you think you--?

Without taking his eyes from KATRINE, AHRMAN hurls a blast of magical energy at NICHOLAS. Unprepared, NICHOLAS is thrown across the room. He hits the wall and bounces to the floor, stunned.

PETER

Uncle Nick!!!

FATALISM

As PETER rushes to NICHOLAS's side, SHARON, JOHNNY and ALDO approach AHRMAN--warily. AHRMAN clubs JOHNNY aside, still staring at KATRINE. KATRINE, meanwhile, has realized something. She dives for the casket--an instant before AHRMAN gets to it. She seizes the CRYSTAL TABLET from inside the casket and dodges back as AHRMAN lunges for her.

KATRINE

(to Nicholas)
We cannot fight him! We must get away from here!

ELSA, armed with the knife that so recently had almost ended her life, has sliced open ALDO's arm. SHARON knocks her away and prevents her from killing him. ELSA charges at SHARON, and so begins a desperate struggle. Still in a trance, ELSA is now attempting to plunge the blade into SHARON. SHARON is losing the struggle, for ELSA's trance has given her fearsome strength.

NICHOLAS, on his feet again, realizes that KATRINE is right, they can't fight AHRMAN when they're so ill-prepared and unarmed.

NICHOLAS

We've got to get past him to the door.

AHRMAN is slowly circling the table on which the casket sits.

AHRMAN

(to Katrine)
Give me the tablet and the orb, bitch.

KATRINE says nothing. She moves around the table, keeping it between her and AHRMAN.

PETER, meanwhile, has gone to SHARON'S rescue, armed with one of the hammers that was sitting on the table. He charges at ELSA, just seconds away from winning her struggle with SHARON and plunging the knife into her stomach.

PETER brings the hammer down on ELSA's wrist and the knife goes flying. SHARON punches ELSA in the jaw and sends her sprawling.

NICHOLAS, KATRINE, JOHNNY and ALDO (ALDO still bleeding) are attempting a diversion to enable them all to get to the door. Between the four of them, they've managed to lift the heavy stone casket lid. Combining their strengths, they heave the lid at AHRMAN. But he's too quick. With a wave of his hand, the stone lid freezes in mid-air for a moment--then reverses direction, rocketing directly for those who heaved it. NICHOLAS, KATRINE and JOHNNY manage to dive to safety, but ALDO is squashed dead against the wall by the heavy projectile.

ELSA is up on her feet again, but PETER (with the hammer) and SHARON (now holding the knife) are keeping her at bay. AHRMAN strides to the lab-bench behind which NICHOLAS and KATRINE have dived. AHRMAN grips the bench and wrenches it up, ripping it right out of the floor to which it was secured. NICHOLAS and KATRINE's hiding-place is gone. AHRMAN sees them crouched there, NICHOLAS holding a pitifully small weapon. AHRMAN laughs victoriously.

What AHRMAN doesn't know is that NICHOLAS's weapon is a fire-extinguisher. NICHOLAS pulls back the lever, aiming the nozzle directly at AHRMAN. White foam hits AHRMAN's face and eyes, blinding him. With a bellow of rage, he tosses the lab-bench aside, clutches at his eyes. NICHOLAS keeps on spraying him.

ELSA, seeing her master's predicament, rushes to his aid. NICHOLAS blasts her in the face, too.

NICHOLAS

(to the others)
Run! Get out now! Get to the van!

SHARON seizes PETER's hand and pulls him to the doorway--where they see RONIM THE DOG standing in the corridor, terrified. NICHOLAS tosses the empty fire-extinguisher aside and pushes KATRINE and JOHNNY ahead of him towards the door. AHRMAN and ELSA are clawing the foam from their faces, blind and disoriented. Screaming with fury, AHRMAN hurls blasts of energy indiscriminately around the room. One of these blasts explodes into JOHNNY's back, killing him instantly.

SHARON, PETER, KATRINE, NICHOLAS, and RONIM THE DOG escape.

DISSOLVE TO:

41 - <u>EXT. BIANCHI HOUSE - ESTABLISHING SHOT - MORNING</u>

The house is affluent but unpretentious, peacefully secluded...

KATRINE (O.S.)
I feel as though I'm trapped in a nightmare.

42 - <u>INT. BIANCHI HOUSE, KITCHEN - MORNING</u>

KATRINE (CONT'D)
I keep praying that I will wake up.

NICHOLAS, KATRINE and SHARON are sitting around a kitchen table with a mostly uneaten breakfast spread out before them. PETER is standing at the counter, spooning table-scraps into a bowl for RONIM.

KATRINE (CONT'D)
(to Nicholas)
I still cannot believe that you are not my Alexander.

NICHOLAS stares into her eyes gravely.

NICHOLAS
You <u>must</u> trust me.
(beat)
Please...can you tell us now what your name is?

KATRINE

(totally bemused)

...Katrine...

PETER

Hey, cool name. I had a crush once on a girl named Katrine. Well--Katrina. She was the first girl who ever let me...

PETER trails off as he sees his uncle giving him a look.

NICHOLAS

(to Katrine)

Katrine...can you tell us...what is the year--the year as you know it?

KATRINE

What?

NICHOLAS

The year. What year is it--as far as you're aware?

KATRINE

I don't... The Y-Year of Our Lord... 1005...

NICHOLAS and SHARON look at one another.

PETER

1005... Holy shit...

KATRINE

T-Tell me...what is the year...as far as you are aware...?

NICHOLAS hesitates, glances uncomfortably again at SHARON.

SHARON

(carefully)

It's <u>2</u>005, Katrine. AD <u>2</u>005...

KATRINE

(eyes wide, staring)

The vehicle we traveled in last night... Your home... Everything <u>in</u> your home...

(beat)

I can't believe... It's not possible...

Suddenly: the DISTANT SOUND OF AN ENGINE. KATRINE looks at the kitchen window through which a JET AIRPLANE can be seen soaring across the sky.

<u>*CLOSE-UP ON*</u> *KATRINE's stunned expression.*

43 - <u>EXT. BIANCHI HOUSE, PATIO - MORNING</u>

NICHOLAS, KATRINE, SHARON and PETER are sitting outside, coffee cups on the table in front of them. RONIM is lying at KATRINE's feet. KATRINE's cheeks are wet with tears.

KATRINE

And that's...the last thing I remember...

NICHOLAS

So, when you let go of the rope, you must have fallen...been knocked unconscious...

SHARON

You know...if we had found you walking on the street and you'd told us the story you just did, we would've been <u>certain</u> you'd escaped from a mental institution--!

NICHOLAS

But the truth is--we found you at the bottom of the sea, inside a casket within a rock-solid cocoon hundreds of years old. A casket we found near a shipwreck is also hundreds of years old...

PETER

Maybe it was magic. It must be magic...

NICHOLAS

No. I believe this is way beyond magic.

NICHOLAS sets a metallic briefcase on the table. Opens it.

NICHOLAS

These are some of the artifacts that were found in the ship's wreckage--prior to the casket being found.
(beat)
Do you recognize this?

NICHOLAS hands KATRINE an ancient, rusted DAGGER. There is a distinctive letter "A" decorating the hilt. KATRINE gasps.

KATRINE

This...is Alexander's...!
(pause)
I saw it just...last night...

Her face turns gray. It starts to tremble from within...

KATRINE

Then it's...true...
(beat)
My whole world...everyone... My father... my mother... Alexander...

NICHOLAS--a little awkwardly--puts his arm around her. She buries her face against his chest. After a few heart-breaking moments:

NICHOLAS

Can I...I need to ask you a couple of things...

KATRINE doesn't respond. NICHOLAS removes the TABLET from the briefcase.

NICHOLAS

You told us about getting back the crystal tablets that had been stolen.
(pause)
Stupid question--but, this is one of those tablets?

After a moment, KATRINE nods.

NICHOLAS

Do you have any idea why...why it was put in the casket with you?

KATRINE shakes her head. Then:

KATRINE

But where are the other two? There are supposed to be <u>three</u>...

NICHOLAS shakes his head, shrugging.

NICHOLAS

What did...Marcus?...tell you about the tablets? Do you remember what he said?

KATRINE

Of <u>course,</u> I remember. It was only yest--
(purses her lips)
Of course, I remember. Marcus said that the tablets are sacred. Ancient. The key...to an immense power. That is why it was so important for us to get them away from Ahrman...

She trails off, her eyes misting over... After a tactful pause:

NICHOLAS

And you're convinced that that guy who attacked us last night...was <u>Ahrman</u>...?

KATRINE

I don't know... It has to be. He's changed his face, his physical form, but...his powers...his voice... I'm sure it was him!
(pause)
Somehow he's followed me--<u>here</u>...

SHARON

Can you think why the dog was in the casket with you?

KATRINE

He's called Ronim.
(pause)
No. I can't think why he was in the casket with me. I can't think why <u>I</u> was in the casket!

PETER

How do you think you and Ronim survived in the casket? Why didn't you die as soon as the oxygen was used up? Why didn't you get old--?

KATRINE

I don't know... I don't know...
(pause)
Unless...

NICHOLAS

Yes...?

KATRINE

(touches the ORB)

Marcus always wore this. He used to tell us that it <u>protected</u> him. I never fully understood how...

(pause)

Maybe it was the orb that kept Ronim and me alive...

(beat)

Maybe it was the orb that somehow enabled me to learn your language...to speak it from the moment I awoke...without even realizing that's what I'm doing...

(pause)

I just don't know... Marcus is always so secretive about things...

NICHOLAS

This...Marcus. Who exactly was he?

Tears sparkle in KATRINE's eyes. She tries to smile.

KATRINE

He was our teacher. Our friend.

(pause)

He was your best friend...

RONIM whimpers under the table as if in agreement about MARCUS.

SHARON

That woman with...Ahrman...last night--did you recognize her?

KATRINE

(shakes her head)

I have never seen her before. Maybe she is one of his new soldiers.

PETER

Wow.

NICHOLAS gets to his feet, draining his cup of coffee.

NICHOLAS

Well, if he's going to be recruiting soldiers, I think we'd better find out more about these tablets and the orb <u>fast</u>. Before he makes his next move...

44 - <u>EXT. UNIVERSITY OF NAPLES - ESTABLISHING SHOT - AFTERNOON</u>

A sign declares that this is the "UNIVERSITY OF NAPLES"...

45 - <u>INT. UNIVERSITY OF NAPLES, ARCHEOLOGICAL ARTIFACT DATING LABORATORY - AFTERNOON</u>

PROFESSOR MANDERS, an elderly woman, is hunched over a microscope which is connected to a SCANNING DEVICE. Within the CRYSTAL TABLET is being scanned. NICHOLAS and PETER are waiting anxiously for the results.

PROFESSOR MANDERS

Of course, the Sub-Atomic Analyzer still has to be properly tested on a wide range of materials. The trials we've conducted have been somewhat limited, as you know...

PROFESSOR MANDERS looks up from the microscope.

PROFESSOR MANDERS (CONT'D)

Well. Without further testing, the accuracy is hardly pinpoint--
(beat)
But the range I can give you is between 4,000 and 5,000 years old.

PETER

WOW! This thing must be worth a fortune, Uncle Nick.

NICHOLAS

About the carved symbols and characters inscribed into the tablet's surface. Do you have <u>any</u> idea what language they represent? Or even what family of languages?

PROFESSOR MANDERS

Unfortunately, no. That's somewhat out of my realm of expertise.

(beat)

Still--you may be in luck nonetheless...

NICHOLAS looks at her questioningly.

PROFESSOR MANDERS (CONT'D)

I would say that you've found this artifact at <u>just</u> the right time. We have visiting us here at the University a learned historian and archeologist from England: Dr. Cornelius Oliver. He's affiliated with the British Museum of Mankind. He's here for two weeks to give a series of lectures--

NICHOLAS

Riiight... I was hoping to attend one of his talks.

PROFESSOR MANDERS

He's an expert on ancient civilizations. <u>And</u> on ancient languages. If anyone can help you, it will be Dr. Oliver.

(pause)

I'd say, Nicholas, that Fate is certainly smiling on you today...

46 - <u>EXT. STREET - AFTERNOON</u>

With the University of Naples in the background, NICHOLAS and PETER are standing beside a motorcycle, preparing to don their helmets. Suddenly, a jeep drives by--

47 - <u>INT. JEEP - THAT MOMENT</u>

ELSA, still in a trance, is at the wheel; AHRMAN is in the passenger seat. AHRMAN and ELSA have both spotted NICHOLAS and PETER.

ELSA

Isn't that--?!

AHRMAN

Yes! Turn this vehicle--<u>now</u>!

ELSA wrenches the wheel, and the jeep makes a SCREECHING U-turn.

48 - <u>EXT. STREET - THAT MOMENT</u>

The SCREECH of the jeep's tires causes NICHOLAS and PETER to look up with a start.

PETER

Uncle Nick...

NICHOLAS

I see them. GET ON!

They both leap onto the motorcycle, PETER behind NICHOLAS. Within seconds, they're speeding away--with the jeep in hot pursuit.

The streets of Naples are far from empty at this time of day. NICHOLAS tries his best to weave the motorcycle through the dense traffic--but AHRMAN and ELSA have no such concern for anyone else's safety. The jeep thunders after the motorcycle. Other cars swerve out of the way, jump up onto the sidewalk, crash into each other, crash into shop windows. One vehicle explodes like a missile into a crowded sidewalk café, sending tables, chairs and people flying. SCREAMS and the HONKING OF HORNS fill the air.

The street is clearing fast between the motorcycle and the pursuing jeep. AHRMAN reaches through the side window and flings a BOLT of supernatural energy forward. It misses NICHOLAS and PETER by mere inches, smashing instead into a street-sign. The motorcycle swerves.

FATALISM

NICHOLAS

Hold on!

PETER holds on to his uncle tightly as they lean into a sweeping turn. The motorcycle is on a smaller street now. With a twist of the throttle, the vehicle leaps forward. PETER cranes his neck around.

PETER

Did we lose th--?

The answer comes in the form of another magical ENERGY BLAST that nearly grazes the top of their helmets. It explodes into the side of a house. People run, screaming, as the jeep screeches into the turn, still hot on the motorcycle's tail.

NICHOLAS makes another turn, barely avoiding another deadly BLAST. They're on a narrower street now, deserted except for a number of big garbage bins. Behind the motorcycle, the jeep makes the turn too. In the distance can be heard the growing WAIL OF SIRENS.

His face contorted with fury, AHRMAN hurls BLAST AFTER BLAST of supernatural energy--but not at the motorcycle, at the garbage bins. The heavy metal containers, surrounded by crackling energy, jump and bounce and roll into the motorcycle's path. Only through skillful handling of the motorcycle does NICHOLAS manage to avoid a collision and a fatal crash. But AHRMAN's jeep is still closing in fast--

NICHOLAS

Pete! Knees and elbows in--NOW!!

PETER

Huh--?

NICHOLAS

Make yourself as narrow as you can! Right! NOW!!!

The motorcycle takes a very sharp, very unexpected turn. It's not so much an alley-way as it is a narrow gap between two buildings. There are bare inches to spare on each side of them.

Because of the abruptness of the turn, AHRMAN and ELSA overshoot the gap. They're forced to stop, reverse, and that's when AHRMAN realizes that the space between the two buildings is much too narrow for the jeep to enter. With a BELLOW OF RAGE, AHRMAN hurls one, two, three BLASTS of energy after the speeding motorcycle--

But NICHOLAS and PETER are now too far ahead. Before the BLASTS can reach them, they make yet another turn into the maze of streets and disappear from view...

49 - <u>INT. BIANCHI HOUSE, LIVING ROOM - AFTERNOON</u>

NICHOLAS and PETER burst in, startling SHARON, who is busy examining sheets of tracing paper on which she had previously (before NICHOLAS and PETER left earlier) made charcoal RUBBINGS of the inscribed surface of the CRYSTAL TABLET.

SHARON

What's happened?

NICHOLAS

Ahrman attacked us. We gave him the slip, but who knows how much time we have before he finds us again.

(beat)

Where's Katrine?

The SOUND OF A DOOR HANDLE TURNING. All heads swivel as KATRINE steps into the room, RONIM by her side. She is dressed in shorts and a T-shirt. She looks clean, scrubbed--and stunningly beautiful.

PETER

(whispering to Nicholas)
Hey--that's <u>my</u> shirt. <u>And</u> my shorts.

SHARON

Sorry--that's all we could find here that would fit.

KATRINE

I heard Ahrman's name mentioned. Where is he now?

NICHOLAS is mesmerized by KATRINE's beauty; he can't take his eyes off her.

NICHOLAS

(clearing his throat)
We ditched him in the city. But I don't think it's safe to stick around here much longer. We've got to stay at least one step ahead of him.
(pause)
We've got an appointment to see Dr. Oliver at the museum this evening. I'm hoping he can give us some information about the tablets and the orb.
(pause)
But what about you, how are you feeling? Have you eaten something yet?

KATRINE

Please...do not be concerned about me.
(pause)
I have been trying...to come to terms with all that you've told me. That...I am no longer in my own...
(fights the tremor in her voice)
I do not know how this has come to be. I do not know why you
(looks at Nicholas)
are the twins of my Alexander. I do not know what manner of sorcery has brought all this about. As much as my wits tell me that none of this can be happening...I would be a fool to doubt the evidence of my own eyes and ears.

(pause)

There is something I need to do, though. Something I need to do that will convince _me_ once and for all; that will enable me to...to mourn...

(fighting to stay composed)

I need to go home.

NICHOLAS's eyes are riveted to KATRINE, gleaming with admiration.

NICHOLAS

Go..._home_...?

KATRINE

To my family's home. My father's castle.

SHARON glances awkwardly at NICHOLAS.

SHARON

But surely...after _ten centuries_...?

KATRINE

If my father's castle is in ruins, then I must _see_ that. If it is no longer there at all--then _I must see that too_.

(meets Nicholas's eye dead-on)

I must see for myself what is--or _isn't_--left of my world.

NICHOLAS

I understand. I promise you I will do everything in my power to make that happen.

(beat)

But right now, we _must_ get out of here.

NICHOLAS goes to the nearby closet and removes something hidden at the back of the top shelf: a hand-gun.

PETER

Hey--I never knew you had one of those!

NICHOLAS

Only for emergencies.

(pause)

Okay, let's round up some clothing and supplies.

(pause)

I get the feeling we won't be coming back here for some time...

50 - <u>EXT. MUSEUM OF NAPLES - ESTABLISHING SHOT - EVENING</u>

The museum is an imposing classical edifice...

51 - <u>INT. MUSEUM OF NAPLES - THAT MOMENT</u>

NICHOLAS, KATRINE, PETER, SHARON and RONIM are passing through a darkened exhibit room. A sign reads: "DARK AGE AND EARLY MEDIEVAL EUROPE EXHIBIT".

PETER

There. That must be where the security guy said Dr. Oliver's waiting.

At the far end of the exhibit room, faint light spills from a slightly open office door. PETER, SHARON and RONIM move on ahead. Behind them, KATRINE gasps suddenly, stopping in her tracks.

NICHOLAS

What--? What is it?

KATRINE's gaze is fixed on a particular display case. Inside are arranged various items: a metal DRINKING GOBLET and DISH; a LADY's SLIPPER; a CHILD'S WOODEN SPINNING TOP; PART OF A HORSE'S HARNESS...

NICHOLAS

What is it? What are you--?

Inside the case, there is a card that reads: "10ᵗʰ/11ᵗʰ CENTURY".

NICHOLAS

Oh...

KATRINE

I...I... These things... These <u>things</u>...
(beat)
They're--They're... My father used to drink from a goblet just like this! And I had a spinning top like that! And the harness...the <u>harness</u>...
(beat)
Just like my Firebrand's...

Tears have sprung to KATRINE's eyes.

KATRINE

(whispering)
My world...my <u>life</u>...in a <u>museum</u>--

NICHOLAS

I'm sorry, Katrine. I'm so sorry.

Not knowing what else to say, he puts his arm around her...

52 - <u>INT. MUSEUM HALLWAY, JUST OUTSIDE OFFICE DOOR - EVENING</u>

SHARON, PETER and RONIM approach the open door. SHARON pokes her head in as she knocks. <u>SHARON's POV</u>:

53 - <u>INT. MUSEUM OFFICE - THAT MOMENT</u>

Two figures, a MAN and WOMAN, are sitting behind a desk, clearly in the middle of an intimate moment. They look up, startled, at SHARON's knock. Their faces are in shadow in the dimly-lit room.

SHARON

Dr. Oliver--?

The MAN jumps to his feet. The WOMAN busies herself tidying papers.

DR. OLIVER

Umm-- Y-Yes... Yes.
(looks at watch)
Is that the time...?
(looks at the woman)
Thanks so much for your assistance, Miss Martini. I think we've gotten as far as we can get this evening.

MISS MARTINI gathers up her purse and coat and moves to the door.

MISS MARTINI

I will see you tomorrow morning then, Dr. Oliver?

DR. OLIVER

Of course, yes. Um, Miss Martini--
(beat)
On your way out--please--the lights...?

MISS MARTINI turns on the overhead lights, then leaves the office, just as SHARON, PETER and RONIM enter. At that moment, NICHOLAS and KATRINE appear in the doorway. DR. OLIVER steps forward into the light to shake SHARON's hand. We see immediately that he is the spitting image of MARCUS, who drowned to death along with PRINCE ALEXANDER, one thousand years ago!

CLOSE-UP ON KATRINE's FACE as she sees him: her eyes widen and her mouth drops open.

CLOSE-UP ON DR. OLIVER's FACE as he turns to KATRINE: his attention is caught by her left hand, frozen in the motion of dabbing at her eye with a tissue. DR. OLIVER's eyes widen and his mouth drops open too...

54 - <u>INT. BIANCHI HOUSE, LIVING ROOM - EVENING</u>

The house has been totally ransacked. AHRMAN stands beside ELSA: his face a mask of anger, her eyes still <u>red</u>, entranced.

                              ELSA

They could return at any moment. We should leave.

                             AHRMAN

This...<u>Bianchi</u>...has <u>my</u> artifacts. They must be here.

AHRMAN is holding a TRACING PAPER RUBBING of the CRYSTAL TABLET's inscribed surface--it's one that SHARON had made earlier, then rejected for some reason, crumpled, and threw in the waste-basket. AHRMAN found it there and smoothed it out.

                              ELSA

You found that rubbing at least. He must have taken the other things with him.
(pause)
I really think we should go--

AHRMAN ignores ELSA: he has recognized something on the RUBBING. He looks closer.

                              ELSA

Please, they could return at any--

                             AHRMAN

Shut--

He waves his hand at ELSA, sends her <u>flying across the room</u>. She slams against the wall, then hangs there, magically pinned.

AHRMAN (CONT'D)

--UP!

ELSA is clearly struggling against AHRMAN's hypnotic control. The red briefly fades from her eyes.

ELSA

Please. Let me go. I want to go home. I need to go home. My babies. My husband--

(beat)

<u>Please</u>!

AHRMAN approaches ELSA, stands in front of her. Fixes her with his blazing gaze.

AHRMAN

Tell me. What is it that you are named?

ELSA

(trance returning)

E-Elsa.

AHRMAN

Elsa. Yes.

(pause)

Tell me...Elsa. What do you believe these people will do to learn the secret of my crystal tablets?

Under AHRMAN's stare, ELSA has lost the struggle of wills. Her eyes slowly become red again as the trance once more overwhelms her.

ELSA

They...They may attempt research. At a library. On the Internet. Perhaps a museum...

AHRMAN considers this, staring at the TABLET RUBBING. His POV shows the charcoal depiction of the CRYSTAL TABLET, with all its inscribed symbols and characters. In one of the triangle's corners is a symbol resembling the spread wingspan of a bird in flight...

DISSOLVE TO:

55 - INT. MUSEUM OFFICE - EVENING

The symbol on the TABLET RUBBING visually DISSOLVES into the identical symbol--KATRINE's BIRTHMARK--seen in CLOSE-UP on the back of her left hand, which is resting on the desk-top. As we take this in, we HEAR:

DR. OLIVER (O.S.)

Good boy. Good boy. Yes--good dog, there's a good dog...

NICHOLAS, KATRINE, SHARON and PETER are seated around the desk, on which lies the metallic briefcase, closed. RONIM is sitting on DR. OLIVER's lap, licking his face...

DR. OLIVER

I think it's clear this little fellow also believes he recognizes me...

PETER

This is so weird! Katrine and Ronim think you're this Marcus guy. And you think you recognize Katrine--

DR. OLIVER

(staring at Katrine)
It's astonishing. Absolutely astonishing.

(shakes his head)
A casket...under the sea...
(shakes his head again)
Absolutely astonishing.

NICHOLAS

Please. You must tell us. Where do you believe you've seen Katrine before?

DR. OLIVER

I--I can't say. Not yet. It's a very complicated story.
(pause)
I will tell you, though, that it involves a painting...

SHARON

A <u>painting</u>? What does--?

KATRINE

(interrupting)
I feel as though I'm going <u>insane</u>! Why has this happened to me?! Why are you
and Alexander both <u>here</u>--but both <u>not</u>...
(clenches her fists)
Oh <u>God</u>!

DR. OLIVER

I'm so sorry. I wish I knew what to say...
(pause)
This is so...<u>remarkable</u>. That you would come to see me...
(to Nicholas)
I'm sorry. I haven't yet given you a chance to explain properly. What exactly
brought you to me today? What did you want to ask me?

*NICHOLAS opens the briefcase on the desk. Inside can be seen THE CRYSTAL ORB,
THE DAGGER, THE CRYSTAL TABLET, as well as TRACING PAPER RUBBINGS, identical
to the one AHRMAN now has.*

NICHOLAS

In the casket with Katrine was this crystal tablet. This orb was around her neck. We're wondering if, somehow, these objects can reveal where Katrine was being taken--and <u>why</u>--when her ship went down--

DR. OLIVER

(sitting forward)
Good <u>God</u>...

With trembling hands, DR. OLIVER takes the ORB and the TABLET from the briefcase. His face is flushed, his eyes filling with tears.

DR. OLIVER

Oh. Oh...

NICHOLAS

You know what these things are?

DR. OLIVER

I-- Yes. I--I didn't think I would ever... that they would ever be found... The orb...the tablets...

KATRINE

So you're aware that there should be more than one tablet?

DR. OLIVER

Yes. <u>Yes</u>. Three. There are three.
(pause)
The other two were found a long, long time ago. By monks--

SHARON

Monks?

DR. OLIVER

Yes. Their monastery is on the outskirts of the city, close to the coast.
According to the story, the discovery seemed to be some sort of Act of God...
 (pause)
Brother Antony--he is the current "keeper" of the tablets, if you will--got
in touch with me about fifteen years ago. He'd heard of me, you see, my
reputation...
 (pause)
Anyway, he requested that I examine the tablets and attempt to decipher the
inscriptions.

NICHOLAS

And could you?

DR. OLIVER

Well... Yes--and no. You see...
 (pause)
No. I think that is all I should tell you for the moment. Any more and you'll
think me a crazy old fool.

KATRINE

But--

DR. OLIVER

Tomorrow we will visit the monastery. Brother Antony will tell you all that
we know. And you will see what I have seen...
 (pause)
In the meantime, I think it's best--from all that you've told me--if you take
rooms tonight in the hotel at which I'm staying. I don't believe you'd be safe
going home...

56 - <u>EXT. THE HOTEL CASTELLO - ESTABLISHING SHOT - NIGHT</u>

A magnificent HOTEL towering on the crest of a hill...

57 - <u>INT. THE HOTEL CASTELLO, KATRINE AND SHARON'S ROOM - NIGHT</u>

SHARON emerges from the bathroom, ready for bed. KATRINE has yet to change; she is sitting on the end of the bed, wide eyes transfixed by the flickering TV screen. SHARON sees that KATRINE is watching a television EVANGELIST striding about a stage, microphone in hand.

EVANGELIST

--and we must <u>pray</u> to the Almighty for forgiveness and guidance! Pray for Him to rescue us from the <u>fiery</u> pits of <u>Hell</u>...! For that is <u>surely</u> where we're all headed, friends, as this miserable new millennium unfolds...! Can there be any doubt that the entire <u>world</u> is heading down a steep, slippery slope towards self-annihilation--towards eternal DAM-nation...?!

SHARON

We'd better get some sleep. We've got an early start tomorrow.
(pause)
Do you remember which is the POWER button?

KATRINE examines the remote control in her hand, then presses a button. She is startled when the TV shuts off.

SHARON

I've left all your toiletries on the bathroom counter for you. Let me know if anything needs explaining.

KATRINE

Thank you. You've been very good to me.

At the bathroom door, KATRINE turns back to SHARON. The young princess looks troubled, almost angry.

KATRINE

(*indicating the TV*)

What that man said. About the world being...on a slope towards...eternal damnation...

SHARON

Mmm?

KATRINE

Is it true?

SHARON

Well...

(*long pause*)

In a lot of ways...I suppose I'd have to say...<u>yes</u>...

KATRINE

(*disgusted*)

So many centuries have gone by. So much progress made. Yet so <u>little</u> has really changed...

SHARON

The world is a God-less place, no doubt about that. No one believes in anything anymore...

58 - <u>EXT. MONASTERY - ESTABLISHING SHOT - MORNING</u>

The monastery is an ancient building situated near a secluded coastal inlet. SHARON's jeep and NICHOLAS's motorcycle seem out of place parked in its courtyard.

BROTHER ANTONY (V.O.)

What a pleasure to see you again, Cornelius.

59 - <u>INT. MONASTERY, BROTHER ANTONY'S STUDY - THAT MOMENT</u>

BROTHER ANTONY (CONT'D)

(embracing Dr. Oliver)

It has been a long time.

DR. OLIVER

Much too long, Antony, much too long.

DR. OLIVER steps aside as NICHOLAS, KATRINE, PETER, SHARON and RONIM enter behind him. BROTHER ANTONY's study is impressive: bookshelves line three of the high-ceilinged walls; on the fourth wall, seen OUT OF FOCUS behind BROTHER ANTONY, is a magnificent painting at least ten feet tall.

DR. OLIVER

Please, let me introduce my friends. Nicholas. Sharon. Peter.

(pause)

And...<u>Katrine</u>.

KATRINE is the last to come forward. As BROTHER ANTONY--an elderly man with thin, white hair--takes her hand, he smiles at her. His eye is caught by her left hand, fiddling with a button on her blouse. His smile fades. His eyes widen. His mouth drops open. He looks at DR. OLIVER. Then back at KATRINE's left hand. Then he turns and stares at the huge painting hanging behind him.

<u>SEEN IN FOCUS</u>: The painting is very old, stylized, typical of the Medieval era, yet somehow more <u>realistic</u> than would be expected for a painting from that time period. It depicts a YOUNG WOMAN, inside a vertical rectangle. Her closed eyes and hands crossed on her breast indicate that she is actually supposed to be <u>lying down</u>, the vertical rectangle surrounding her in reality a <u>horizontal box</u> rendered without visual perspective. Next to the box, one underneath the other, are <u>three triangles</u>.

KATRINE moves slowly towards the painting. She looks as shocked as BROTHER ANTONY.

KATRINE

Look--

*She shows the others the birthmark on the back of her hand. Then points out
the identical symbol on the LEFT HAND of the WOMAN IN THE PAINTING, and in
the corner of each of the THREE PAINTED TRIANGLES.*

*Quickly, NICHOLAS opens his metallic briefcase and removes the CRYSTAL TABLET.
(Not quite knowing why, he also removes the TRACING PAPER RUBBINGS OF THE
CRYSTAL TABLET and folds them into his jacket pocket.) Tears spring to BROTHER
ANTONY's eyes, tears of astonishment, recognition. NICHOLAS holds the TABLET
up beside the painting.*

NICHOLAS

There.
(points)
There it is!

*CLOSE-UP ON THE CRYSTAL TABLET: There, in the same corner as on each PAINTED
TRIANGLE, can be seen the symbol of a bird's spread wingspan...*

PETER

Wow...

KATRINE

(wonderingly)
Th-This is...me. Inside the casket you found me in. I-I'm... This is me...!

BROTHER ANTONY

You were found? In a casket?

NICHOLAS

Yes... At the bottom of the sea. Just off-shore, a mile or so south of here...

BROTHER ANTONY

Oh my. Oh my. <u>Oh my oh my oh my</u>...

NICHOLAS

Brother Antony? What is-- What can you tell us about this painting?

BROTHER ANTONY seems overcome by what's happening. He pulls himself unsteadily into a seat. He's staring at KATRINE in awe-struck wonder.

BROTHER ANTONY

This is... This is... I--I don't know what to say...

SHARON

What is it? What do you know about this painting, Brother?

BROTHER ANTONY struggles to compose himself.

BROTHER ANTONY

I--I'm sorry. Your coming here...it has quite taken me by surprise.

He stares openly at KATRINE, eyes wide.

BROTHER ANTONY

I'll tell you what I know...
(long pause)
When I--When I first came here, as a young man, I was told that there was...a legend associated with this monastery. A legend dating back many hundreds of years, that had been passed down, through the centuries. The legend told of a night, not long after the monastery was built--a night when there was a terrible, terrible storm. Part of the monastery's roof was damaged--the storm was that violent.
(pause)
In the morning, once the storm had spent itself, the beach of our little inlet here was strewn with debris from the wreckage of a sailing vessel. Clinging

to one of these pieces of debris, very near death, was a man. The monks who found him brought him inside to attempt to revive him.

(pause)

The man lingered near death for days. He was feverish, delirious, badly injured. And some days later, he succumbed to his injuries.

(pause)

But before he died, in the brief periods that he was lucid, he told the monks what had happened.

(pause)

He was, he said, the Captain of the ship that had been wrecked in the storm. They had been sailing east when the storm hit.

(stares at Katrine)

The Captain said that on board the ship was a young princess, trapped in a perpetual sleep... He described the princess in detail, even down to the birthmark on her hand.

(pause)

He said they were on their way to a...a Holy Sanctuary...in a land far from their home. That they had been directed to this destination by the scriptures inscribed on three crystal tablets.

(stares at tablet)

The tablets, he said, also bore the same symbol found on the princess's hand. There was some connection there, but he didn't know what.

(pause)

The Captain believed that when the ship went down, the sleeping princess went down as well.

(pause)

The monks were so moved by the Captain's story that after he died, they recorded what he had told them. They recorded it in the form of a painting.

(indicates the wall)

<u>This</u> painting--

NICHOLAS

But how did the monks know they weren't just listening to the...the ramblings of a dying man?

BROTHER ANTONY

It wasn't the first time, you see, that they had heard of this Holy Sanctuary. Throughout the recorded history of Christianity--indeed, the recorded history of most of the world's established religions--there have been stories, legends, of a holy place, a heavenly sanctuary <u>right here on earth</u>...
(*pause*)
But there was far more tangible evidence: you see, the Captain had managed to salvage something from the wreckage of his ship.
(*pause*)
He had with him <u>two of the three crystal tablets</u>...

60 - <u>**INT. MONASTERY, BASEMENT - MORNING**</u>

This basement room is cavernous, furnished with row upon row of ten-foot high oak bookcases--all of them empty. The group is now gathered between the second and third-last bookcases of the last row. NICHOLAS and BROTHER ANTONY are kneeling beside each other, the others facing them across a particular flagstone in the floor. The MONK is running his hands over the stone.

BROTHER ANTONY

This...Yes, I'm sure this is the one.
(*fingers feel along the edge of the stone*)
Yes--<u>there</u>--
(to Nicholas)
Feel along the other edge. You should find a series of grooves.

NICHOLAS's fingers find the grooves, and he and BROTHER ANTONY manage to lift the heavy stone up and set it aside. Inside the exposed cavity is a <u>small stone chest</u>. As BROTHER ANTONY reaches into the hole, we HEAR <u>OFF-SCREEN</u> the SOUND OF RONIM GROWLING.

DR. OLIVER

Quiet, boy.

The chest is laid on the stone floor and opened. There, arranged on a satin pillow, are the SECOND AND THIRD CRYSTAL TABLETS. And RONIM's GROWLING is getting louder--

NICHOLAS
(to Ronim)
Will you be quiet--

MALE VOICE (O.S.)
I believe the animal is attempting to warn you.

TWO FIGURES wearing hooded monk's robes move into view. The smaller of the two is holding a gun.

BROTHER ANTONY
Brothers--what is the meaning of this?

KATRINE still hasn't turned to face the intruders.

TALLER INTRUDER
Are you not going to face me--princess? Will you not look in the eye the one whose life you and your thieving friends attempted to destroy?

KATRINE's eyes lock on NICHOLAS's. Silently, she mouths a single word:

KATRINE
Ahrman.

No one moves for a long moment. Then the SHORTER INTRUDER pulls back the hood from her head.

ELSA
Please. Do not resist. I do not want to use this weapon--

AHRMAN pulls off his own hood.

AHRMAN

Look at me--princess! LOOK AT ME!!

Moving lightning-fast, KATRINE suddenly reaches down into the open chest. She pulls her hand back--with nothing in it--and slams the lid shut. Then she dives through two shelves in the bookcase beside her. By the time AHRMAN reacts--believing she's taken the TABLETS--and goes after her, she is already diving through the next bookcase.

AHRMAN

--Bring them back--bitch--!

As ELSA turns slightly to see where KATRINE has gone, SHARON throws herself at ELSA and they both fall to the ground.

PETER

Sharon!!

PETER and SHARON grapple with ELSA to get the gun. Meanwhile, NICHOLAS thrusts his briefcase at DR. OLIVER.

NICHOLAS

Lock the two tablets in here with the other one. Try to hide the briefcase somewhere. Quickly.
(to Brother Antony)
Is that all right?

BROTHER ANTONY

Y-Yes--Anything--to keep them safe.

NICHOLAS rushes to SHARON and PETER and, with his help, they manage to take the gun from ELSA. Everyone scrambles to their feet. NICHOLAS hands the gun to SHARON. She points it at ELSA.

SHARON

Stand perfectly still...and perfectly silent...or I swear I'll blow your knee-caps off...

NICHOLAS takes off after AHRMAN, drawing his own gun. AHRMAN is still hunting for KATRINE between the many bookcases. Suddenly, NICHOLAS sees KATRINE, crouched on the top shelf of a bookcase in the first row. AHRMAN has walked right by her.

AHRMAN (O.S.)

The door is locked! There is nowhere to run!

NICHOLAS signals to KATRINE silently. She climbs down off the bookcase and runs to him.

KATRINE

(whispering)
We need to distract him so we can get out of here.

NICHOLAS

I have an idea--

Holstering his gun, NICHOLAS races back with KATRINE to the others. SHARON, PETER and RONIM have ELSA backed up against the wall. NICHOLAS pushes with all his strength against the last ten-foot high bookcase in the row. At the other end of the row, AHRMAN is standing, listening for KATRINE. With KATRINE's and PETER's help, the massive bookcase is tipped over. It crashes into the next bookcase, which crashes into the next one--and so on down the row, like a line of dominoes. The FINAL BOOKCASE is brought down with a THUNDEROUS SMASH.

PETER

YES! He's toast! He's totally toast!

DR. OLIVER and BROTHER ANTONY rush up, DR. OLIVER still gripping the metallic briefcase.

DR. OLIVER

We couldn't find anywhere to--

NICHOLAS

(takes briefcase)
That's okay. We've got to get out of here--<u>now</u>. Who knows how long Ahrman's going to stay down--

Suddenly, a LOW RUMBLE...that BUILDS to a ROAR OF FURY:

AHRMAN

NooooOOOOOO!!!!

The bookcases start to magically, one by one, rise to a standing position again--and then they begin to <u>slide</u>, one bookcase SLAMMING into the next, bearing down on NICHOLAS's group like a hurtling bull-dozer.

KATRINE

Look OUT--!

The bookcases plow into the wall. Everyone barely manages to dive to safety. In the commotion, ELSA knocks the gun out of SHARON's hand, catches it, and thrusts the barrel at SHARON's face.

ELSA

--don't <u>MOVE</u>--!

Abruptly, distracting her, a THUNDERING VOICE:

AHRMAN

THESE GAMES <u>END</u>--

FATALISM

--AHRMAN strides into view--

AHRMAN (CONT'D)

--NOW!!!

Suddenly, <u>all the rows of bookcases</u> are SLAMMED magically aside, left and right, into the walls. SCRAPING, SMASHING SOUNDS fill the air.

NICHOLAS

RUN FOR THE DOOR! RUN--!

They all start to run. ELSA catches up to NICHOLAS. She seizes his wrist, her gun jabbing at his back--

AHRMAN

THESE GAMES END--<u>NOW</u>!!

There is a bizarre EXPLOSION in the room, like a MUTED THUNDERCLAP. Everyone--except for AHRMAN--is blown up into the air. As they're tossed up towards the ceiling, ELSA pulls the trigger of the gun. <u>And that's when everything freezes</u>. Each person is frozen in the air in mid-tumble. NICHOLAS's eyes are locked on the BULLET suspended in the air, <u>four feet away from his chest</u>...

AHRMAN

Your games are <u>ENDED</u>. I will not tolerate any further interference.

We see now that AHRMAN's latest "borrowed" physical form has been transformed forever by decay. Even as he speaks, the rot of his skin and hair and teeth relentlessly progresses.

AHRMAN

In a few moments, <u>Princess Katrine</u>, I will take possession of my belongings. <u>My</u> belongings. Curious, isn't it, that in spite of all your efforts, my orb and my tablets are destined to return to me. Their <u>rightful</u> owner.

(beat)

But I'll allow your friend--this...<u>double</u> for your precious Prince Alexander--to hold them for me--for just a few more minutes.

(beat)

Until I am finished.

AHRMAN waves his rotting hand in a wide arc. Suddenly, BROTHER ANTONY and ELSA are able to move. Slowly, they lower to the floor.

AHRMAN

Bring him to me.

ELSA forces the trembling MONK over to AHRMAN.

BROTHER ANTONY

P-Please--this is a house of God--

AHRMAN

(laughs)

God? Yes, of course. It always comes back to your God, doesn't it?

(pause; snarling)

This situation would have been resolved a <u>millennium</u> ago if I did not have...the <u>difficulty</u> that I do dealing with...so-called "Men of <u>God</u>." Isn't that true, Princess Katrine?

AHRMAN clamps his huge hand on BROTHER ANTONY's shoulder.

AHRMAN (CONT'D)

No difficulty this time, however.

AHRMAN pushes down; BROTHER ANTONY's knees buckle and bend.

AHRMAN (CONT'D)

This time I will take a much more...direct approach...

BROTHER ANTONY is forced to his knees.

61 - <u>INT. MONASTERY, BASEMENT PASSAGEWAY - MORNING</u>

BROTHER DOMENIC and BROTHER FRANCIS are walking past the door to the basement room when a SCREAM OF AGONY makes them almost jump out of their skins.

BROTHER DOMENIC

Dear <u>God</u>--!

BROTHER FRANCIS

Was that...Brother Antony...?

BROTHER DOMENIC tries to open the door but cannot: it isn't locked, but held shut by AHRMAN's magic.

BROTHER DOMENIC

Brother Antony! <u>Brother Antony</u>!

Another SCREAM is heard from behind the door.

BROTHER FRANCIS

What's happening--?!

BROTHER DOMENIC

The police! We must call the police!

BROTHER FRANCIS's hand slips into the folds of his robe and emerges holding a cell-phone. He flips it open and punches out the number...

62 - <u>INT. MONASTERY, BASEMENT - MORNING</u>

<u>CLOSE-UP</u> on BROTHER ANTONY's FACE: the poor man is in AGONY.

BROTHER ANTONY

I am...a man of...<u>God</u>...

AHRMAN

Now where have I heard <u>that</u> before...? You priests are so unimaginative. Not one ounce of originality among the lot of you.
(pause)
Boring and predictable--on the outside...
(pause)
...On the <u>in</u>side...

OUR VIEW WIDENS and we see magical green energy coiling around BROTHER ANTONY. <u>*We also see that the whole top of his skull has been neatly removed, exposing his brain...*</u>

AHRMAN

Now, "Man of God"-- as you call yourself--I will have some information from you.

NICHOLAS, KATRINE, SHARON, PETER, DR. OLIVER and RONIM are still frozen in the air, captive witnesses...

AHRMAN

Tell me the secret of my crystal tablets. Tell me what power it is that they hold.

AHRMAN's fingers <u>plunge into the MONK's exposed brain</u>. The old man's TORTURED SCREAM is bone-chilling.

BROTHER ANTONY

I--I don't-- No one knows for c-certain! It's a legend! It's a legend--not a definite fact!

AHRMAN

Answer me--!

Suddenly, AHRMAN's magic creates A VIRTUAL IMAGE--stolen from BROTHER ANTONY's mind--that fills the basement room, surrounding everyone present: an entire sea of CRASHING WAVES. Tossed on this stormy sea, lashed by a torrential downpour, is an ARK--

BROTHER ANTONY

(panting, moaning)
--and the fountains of the Heavens were... broken open...the entire earth flooded... to cleanse it of corruption, wickedness... evil... PLEASE no--

AHRMAN's grip on the MONK's brain tightens and the poor man SCREAMS IN AGONY. Then:

BROTHER ANTONY

--the only man spared this...terrible fate ...was Noah...a good, holy...man--full of faith. He built an ark...and he and his family...and the animals...they brought with them...were allowed to...survive...

THE ARK rolls on the violent waves--then abruptly the stormy sea dissolves in a flash of green light--to be replaced by an image of the same sea after the downpour, the ARK bobbing on calm waters...

BROTHER ANTONY

(strangled, gasping)
--after forty days and...forty nights... the rain ended--

--Standing on the deck of the ARK is A WHITE-HAIRED MAN. He releases A DOVE into the air--

BROTHER ANTONY
--and Noah sent out a dove...to search for dry land. The bird--PLEASE I CAN'T--

AHRMAN gives the MONK's brain a brutal squeeze--

AHRMAN

CONTINUE--!

BROTHER ANTONY

(breathless with agony)

--the dove...eventually returned...

--we see the DOVE alight on NOAH's outstretched hand--

BROTHER ANTONY

...and in its beak...was an...olive branch ...and Noah knew the...flood waters were receding--

--and the VIRTUAL IMAGE changes again, this time transforming into the summit of a mountain. Perched there is the ARK, from which NOAH and his family and many species of animals are emerging--

BROTHER ANTONY

--the Ark--came to rest...on a mountain-top...and Noah, the faithful one...was told by the Creator...that such absolute ...destruction would never be brought down upon mankind again--

--suddenly, an oval of blinding white light obliterates the image--

BROTHER ANTONY

...as Noah descended from the mountain... he was told that a Guardian...a Sacred Sentinel...was to be left in that place to watch over...the earth. A Holy Sanctuary was created in which...this guardian would reside--

AHRMAN

Where? Where is this sanctuary?

(squeezes the monk's brain eagerly)

WHERE--?!

BROTHER ANTONY

(almost wailing)

I--I don't...I don't...

(pause)

The legend says that...the purpose of the Guardian...this protector for humankind... was to ensure the...eternal cosmic balance between Good...and Evil...would always be maintained. As long as...the Guardian existed...there would always <u>have</u> to be a balance--

(pause)

But if--if the Guardian were ever to be destroyed...then the balance would be destroyed too...and Evil would triumph...

(pause)

Eventually...the world as we know it... would come to an end...

AHRMAN

The Sanctuary, monk--<u>WHERE IS IT</u>?! Will I learn the secret of immortality there--?!

BROTHER ANTONY

I D-DON'T KNOW!

(beat)

The location of the Sanctuary was a closely-guarded secret--

--the <u>oval of blinding white light</u> vanishes; the mountain-top returns. NOAH stands beside the grounded ARK. Suddenly, a bolt of lightning strikes the rocks at his feet. The rocks magically melt together, forming an expanse of <u>crystal</u>--which abruptly <u>shatters</u> into large fragments. <u>THEN THE IMAGE CHANGES</u>. We now see NOAH, seated at a work-table. Before him are three chunks of crystal and in his hands a fourth, which he is working at with some kind of file. The crystal is already taking shape: <u>one of the three holy tablets</u>...

BROTHER ANTONY

--but even though the Sanctuary was a secret, Noah...was instructed to make a permanent record of what the Creator had wrought... That record was said to have been inscribed on the surface of the three crystal tablets--

AHRMAN

And what <u>else</u>?! There is more to it than <u>that</u>--I know it!!

The MONK's SOBS are heart-rending.

BROTHER ANTONY

Please--for the love of--<u>Please</u>...let me <u>die</u>...

AHRMAN

Tell me what else you know--!!

--NOAH slides the file back and forth against the crystal--

BROTHER ANTONY

I--I--

AHRMAN

TELL ME--!!

BROTHER ANTONY

--the f-functions...of the orb...and the tablets...were said to be many-fold...but the main purpose...the main purpose...
(pause)
...the orb and the tablets...according to the legend...serve as <u>the key</u>...the key which will allow entry to the Holy Sanctuary...

AHRMAN is triumphant. Even as a rotting strip of flesh peels away from his forehead...

AHRMAN

And what about the <u>symbol</u>? The symbol of the bird's wings? What purpose does the princess serve in all this?!

BROTHER ANTONY

I--

SUDDENLY, FROM OUTSIDE: THE SOUND OF MANY SIRENS--

AHRMAN

What is that?!

ELSA

It sounds like the police! We should get out of here...

AHRMAN lets go of BROTHER ANTONY's brain. BROTHER ANTONY topples over and hits the floor. The image of NOAH disappears. AHRMAN is clearly a little drained now...

AHRMAN

They will not ruin this! They WILL NOT!
(gestures at Nicholas, etc.)
Guard them!

AHRMAN storms out of the room. At that moment, although everyone and everything are still mostly frozen in the air, there are sudden twitches of movement amidst the group. And the bullet jerks closer to NICHOLAS's chest...

63 - INT. MONASTERY, BASEMENT PASSAGEWAY - MORNING

AHRMAN levitates himself to a high window and sees a swarm of police cars outside, the boots of running officers.

POLICE OFFICER 1 (O.S.)

Halt! Don't move!

AHRMAN turns. At the end of the passage is a group of POLICE OFFICERS. The ones in front have their guns aimed at him. The one in the very front is

POLICE OFFICER 1. All of them look shocked to see AHRMAN levitating in the air--

POLICE OFFICER 1

Put your hands up!

AHRMAN does indeed put one of his hands up. To send a blast of magical energy rocketing down the passage. The OFFICERS dive for safety...but one of them gets his leg blown off below the knee. POLICE OFFICER 1, crouched against the wall now, fires his gun at AHRMAN. AHRMAN raises his fist--and the bullet stops in mid-air. It spins around, then speeds back the way it came. It strikes POLICE OFFICER 1 in the chest, killing him before he hits the floor. AHRMAN rushes to a side-passage, heading for a stairwell.

64 - INT. MONASTERY, BASEMENT - MORNING

The group is still suspended in the air, but it's clear that AHRMAN's freezing spell is wearing off: everyone is now able to move just a little. And the bullet jerks closer to NICHOLAS's heart--

NICHOLAS

B...ull...et...

At that instant, SHARON drops like a stone. Winded, she glances at the door--although standing in the doorway, ELSA has her attention focused down the passageway. SHARON snatches up a broken plank and tosses it up to NICHOLAS. He just manages to catch it. Then, he wrenches his arm into motion and uses the wood to bat away the bullet. This is the exact instant that AHRMAN's spell breaks completely: the SOUND OF THE DELAY-FIRED BULLET STRIKING THE STONE CEILING IS HEARD as everyone falls from the air. They mostly land without injury; except for PETER, who hits the floor awkwardly, his ankle twisting. ELSA hears the commotion and turns--

ELSA

No!!

ELSA runs back into the room. KATRINE dives at her and both women roll to the floor. ELSA loses her gun. NICHOLAS draws his own gun as he's running to KATRINE. KATRINE has ELSA pinned down. SHARON and DR. OLIVER rush to the dying BROTHER ANTONY as the sounds of SCREAMS AND EXPLOSIONS COME FROM OUTSIDE THE MONASTERY.

                          DR. OLIVER

It's all right. We'll get help. Just lie still--

But all three know that death is imminent. Suddenly, BROTHER ANTONY grips DR. OLIVER's hand...

                          BROTHER ANTONY

You must...take our tablets...to safety, with yours. Don't allow him...
(beat)
He must not...get to the Sanctuary. Promise...me. He must be...stopped...
(beat)
Or else...all is lost...

BROTHER ANTONY's violated head falls back. He is on the verge of slipping away--then, his eyes flutter open--

                          BROTHER ANTONY

--<u>hide</u>--

The MONK whispers something to DR. OLIVER. DR. OLIVER nods--and BROTHER ANTONY dies. In the background, KATRINE is pulling ELSA to her feet. Suddenly, there is a DOOMING CRASH directly above them. A hole is being blasted in the ceiling--a growing hole through which can be seen AHRMAN's crazed eyes--

                            AHRMAN

ELSA!
(beat)
My tablets--my orb--the princess! Get them! We are leaving--<u>NOW</u>!!

KATRINE

Run!!

KATRINE shoves ELSA aside. She stumbles, falls. KATRINE and NICHOLAS hurry SHARON, DR. OLIVER, PETER and RONIM out of the room. ELSA struggles to her feet as AHRMAN descends through the hole in the ceiling.

AHRMAN

After them--!!

With ELSA in the lead, they rush to the door--

65 - <u>INT. BASEMENT PASSAGEWAY - THAT MOMENT</u>

To the left of the door, the escaping group is just rounding the corner, limping PETER bringing up the rear.

ELSA

There--!

ELSA and AHRMAN charge after them, when suddenly, from behind:

POLICE OFFICER (O.S.)

FREEZE! Stay right where you are!

AHRMAN swings around. At least EIGHT POLICE OFFICERS are approaching, each armed with a bizarre weapon, like a futuristic BAZOOKA.

POLICE OFFICER

Drop your weapons--!

AHRMAN--who has been expending huge amounts of sorcerous energy over a relatively short period--manages to tap a hidden reserve and shoots a hurtling blast, blowing the arm off a POLICE OFFICER. The other OFFICERS open fire. ELSA slips away to follow NICHOLAS's GROUP...

66 - <u>INT. MAZE OF PASSAGES, FURTHER ON - THAT MOMENT</u>

DR. OLIVER is ahead of everyone as they run.

DR. OLIVER

This way. Brother Antony said it was along here--

They come to a corner. PETER is last and, just before he turns the corner, a hand grabs his collar and <u>yanks him bodily backwards</u>--

67 - <u>INT. NEXT PASSAGE (AROUND THE CORNER) - THAT MOMENT</u>

At the end of this passage: a dead end.

NICHOLAS

Are you sure--?

DR. OLIVER

I think--<u>Yes</u>! There it is--just like he said--

DR. OLIVER hurries over to a small grating set into the stone wall near the floor. He drops to his knees.

KATRINE

Hurry--I don't think we've lost them!

SHARON turns--she is shocked to see that PETER is not there.

SHARON

<u>Pete</u>--?

93

Frantically, she retraces their steps around the corner. At the far end of this passage, already turning the <u>next</u> corner, is PETER, being dragged backwards by ELSA, who has her forearm around his throat.

ELSA

I'll trade him for the tablets and the orb! A simple trade--or I give him to Ahrman--!

SHARON ignores the offer and charges after ELSA. SHARON rips ELSA's arm away from PETER's throat and yanks him free. Then SHARON delivers a hefty right-hook to ELSA's jaw, sending her sprawling to the floor.

SHARON

(to Peter)
Run! Find Nick!

PETER

But--

SHARON

GO!

PETER limps off. SHARON heaves ELSA up into a sitting position. She slaps ELSA hard across the face. For a brief moment, the red <u>flickers and fades</u> from ELSA's eyes.

ELSA

(waking up)
Please, you've got to help me get away from him! <u>Please</u>! My <u>children</u>--I need to get...home to...my...

The red returns to ELSA's eyes as AHRMAN's hypnotic control grips her again. Her mouth twists into a sly smirk. SHARON is stunned by the abrupt, chilling <u>flip-flop-flip</u> that ELSA's personality just went through, so stunned that she *doesn't see ELSA's fingers sliding into the top of her boot, emerging stealthily with a sharp, glinting weapon...*

68 - <u>INT. DEAD-END PASSAGE - THAT MOMENT</u>

DR. OLIVER, kneeling, has his hand and forearm buried in the hole behind the small grating.

DR. OLIVER

Almost...Al...most...<u>There</u>--!

He turns a hidden handle. Suddenly, under KATRINE's FEET: the stones tremble--she jumps off instantly--and a broad section of the floor sinks slowly down and <u>slides out of the way</u>, revealing the top of a crumbling <u>stone stairway</u> descending into darkness--

DR. OLIVER

The sub-basement... They'll never find us...

The SOUNDS of AHRMAN's confrontation with the POLICE are getting louder, as though the battle were drifting <u>towards them</u>...

NICHOLAS

Let's get down there--<u>now</u>--

He motions for KATRINE to go first, then turns, looking for

NICHOLAS

Sharon--? Pete--?

At that moment, PETER appears around the corner, limping.

PETER

Uncle Nick--Sharon--Elsa--Back there!

95

NICHOLAS runs to him, grips his shoulder.

NICHOLAS

Where--? Where's Sharon--?!

PETER

Back this way! Elsa--!

NICHOLAS

No! You stay here. I'll go.

PETER

But--

NICHOLAS

Stay here!

NICHOLAS runs off, still holding the metallic briefcase. DR. OLIVER fits the grating back into position.

KATRINE

(to Peter)
Are you all right--?

PETER

Yes, but--

KATRINE

We have to hurry! Down there--

PETER

But Sharon--!

KATRINE

Pete--Hurry--!

KATRINE ushers PETER to the top step. RONIM is already going down.

KATRINE

Be careful.

KATRINE goes next, then DR. OLIVER, bringing up the rear.

69 - <u>INT. SUB-BASEMENT CUBBY-HOLE - THAT MOMENT</u>

They reach the bottom of the steps, one by one.

KATRINE

We can't close it yet. Not 'til Nicholas and--

DR. OLIVER

What?

KATRINE

Listen--

They listen. The SOUNDS of AHRMAN's battle with the police have suddenly stopped. Then, from out of nowhere...

MAN'S VOICE (O.S.)

<u>Katrine</u>...where are you...?

KATRINE's head jerks up. Her eyes widen.

MAN'S VOICE (O.S.)

<u>Katrine</u>...where <u>are</u> you...?

The expression on KATRINE's face becomes one of <u>recognition</u>. But there is bewilderment as well; and hopeful <u>joy</u>...

KATRINE

F-Father...?

70 - <u>INT. PASSAGEWAY - THAT MOMENT</u>

With a gun in one hand and a briefcase in the other, NICHOLAS dashes through the maze of passages.

NICHOLAS

Sharon--! Sharon--!!

He rounds a corner--and there is SHARON, walking slowly towards him, holding on to her stomach.

NICHOLAS

Sharon...?

She looks at NICHOLAS. She is pale, confused, bewildered.

SHARON

I...

She gasps. Blood spills from her mouth, leaks between her fingers. She stumbles forward, falling. NICHOLAS drops the briefcase and lunges to catch her. Her collapsing weight brings them both to the floor. NICHOLAS cradles her.

NICHOLAS

Sharon--! <u>Sharon</u>--?!!

Silently, ELSA steps behind NICHOLAS. She picks up the metallic briefcase. NICHOLAS starts to turn--<u>but too late</u>. ELSA swings with the briefcase, striking NICHOLAS on the side of the head. He slumps unconscious to the floor.

71 - <u>INT. SUB-BASEMENT CUBBY-HOLE - THAT MOMENT</u>

DR. OLIVER

Katrine--<u>no</u>--!!

KATRINE is scrambling back up the stone steps.

KATRINE

It's my father! My father--!!

She reaches the top of the steps.

DR. OLIVER

It can't be! <u>How</u> can it be--?!

PETER starts to climb up after her, as fast as he can.

PETER

Katrine--wait--!

<u>*And that's when the opening begins to close*</u>*--very, very quickly--*

DR. OLIVER

How--?

PETER launches himself up through the opening after KATRINE--

72 - <u>INT. DEAD-END PASSAGE - THAT MOMENT</u>

--<u>just</u> making it through before the section of floor SLAMS back into place. DR. OLIVER and RONIM are trapped now in the sub-basement. Ahead, KATRINE is disappearing around the corner.

PETER

Katrine--!!

99

73 - <u>INT. PASSAGEWAY (AROUND THE CORNER) - THAT MOMENT</u>

KATRINE comes to an abrupt halt as she sees her father, <u>KING GALEN</u>, up ahead. Confused and overcome with emotion, KATRINE throws herself into his arms, sobbing. Transported with the joy of their reunion, they start to whirl. At that moment, PETER rounds the corner--and freezes. He can see quite clearly that KATRINE is whirling obliviously in the arms of, not her father, but <u>AHRMAN</u>.

PETER

Let go of her!! LET GO OF HER!!
(beat)
Katrine--IT'S AHRMAN! <u>AHRMAN</u>--!!

The joyful whirling stops.

PETER

Katrine--!

KATRINE leans back, far enough to see <u>the grinning, rotted face of the WARLORD AHRMAN</u>--

KATRINE

<u>NOOOO</u>--!!

She struggles violently, uselessly.

AHRMAN

Oh my daughter! My darling daughter!

AHRMAN punches KATRINE in the face, knocking her unconscious. PETER leaps at AHRMAN--but never manages to reach him. The metallic briefcase arcs into the frame, striking PETER in the stomach. He falls to the ground. ELSA steps into view as AHRMAN slings KATRINE over his shoulder.

ELSA

Shall I kill him?

AHRMAN

Later.

(pause)

At the moment, he is more used to me alive...

(pause)

In the event that Princess Katrine needs to be <u>persuaded</u> to answer any of my questions...to do what I tell her to d--

At that moment, AHRMAN notices FOUR DEAD POLICE OFFICERS, lying in an adjoining passage. With KATRINE still on his shoulder, AHRMAN squats down beside each of them. One at a time, he places his hand on the OFFICERS. Magical energy crackles. One at a time, <u>the dead men awaken</u>. They sit up, then stand, picking up their futuristic BAZOOKA weapons. Their eyes are red, staring, entranced...

AHRMAN

(to Elsa)

We're leaving now. Bring the boy.

PETER, horrified at what he's just seen, terrified, screams:

PETER

UNCLE NICK! UNCLE NICK!!

DISSOLVE TO:

74 - <u>EXT. MONASTERY, COURTYARD - EVENING</u>

Standing alongside a stretcher is NICHOLAS, his eyes glazed with a blasted, devastated look, his mouth twisted in a grimace of restrained emotion. DR. OLIVER and RONIM are slightly apart from him, immensely sad. On the stretcher lies SHARON, in a body bag. A MORGUE ATTENDANT zips up the bag as a POLICE INSPECTOR approaches.

INSPECTOR MESSINA

(grim, ashen-faced)

I have never seen anything like this in my entire career. In my entire <u>life</u>...

(shakes his head)

I will need you both in my office tomorrow morning to take your complete statements. In the meantime, we will proceed on the information you've given us, such as it is.

The INSPECTOR moves off to give instructions to one of the other investigators working in the background.

DR. OLIVER

Blaming yourself is not going to help matters, you do see that.

NICHOLAS says nothing.

DR. OLIVER (CONT'D)

Look. I know you want to take responsibility for Sharon's murder and Katrine and Peter's abduction. I'm guessing you even blame yourself for the engine malfunction on your boat that killed your wife and your sister three years ago--don't look at me like that, I talked to Professor Manders about you after I agreed to meet with you yesterday. She told me what you've been through.

102

(pause)

The point is, even though you feel the need to take responsibility for these terrible things...I can say with some assurance that there were other forces at work that had nothing whatsoever to do with you!

NICHOLAS

Like the "Hand of God," you mean?

(beat)

If you're going to give me that "Destiny," "Fate," "Hand of God" crap, you can just...you can just...spare me, okay?

(bitterly)

"Hand of God." My wife, my sister saw the bloody "Hand of God" in everything. Where was God when they really needed him? Tell me that.

NICHOLAS sits on an old stone bench, away from all the activity. DR. OLIVER joins him.

DR. OLIVER

So...if you don't believe in the power of God...I suppose you don't believe any of what we were told...shown...through poor Brother Antony?

NICHOLAS leans forward, covers his face with his hands.

NICHOLAS

I don't...I don't know...

(uncovers his face)

That stuff about a Holy Sanctuary--a Sacred Sentinel--a...cosmic balance between GOOD and EVIL...

(shakes his head)

All that Biblical mumbo-jumbo about Noah's Ark and the Flood! I mean--for centuries, there have been legends about Noah's Ark. It's stuck up on top of Mount Ararat, in Turkey. But there have been scores of expeditions up that mountain! Going all the way back to the Ancient Greeks. And no one's ever found a thing!

DR. OLIVER

Well, maybe Mount Ararat isn't the right location--but that doesn't mean the Ark and the Sanctuary can't be somewhere <u>else</u>...

(pause)

I'll tell you what I believe, shall I? I believe that this Holy Sanctuary <u>does</u> exist. And, one thousand years ago, Katrine was being taken there by her fiancé, Alexander, and their friend, Marcus. To be roused from her coma--maybe. But ultimately for a much larger reason. And then the ship they were on sank.

(pause)

I'm becoming increasingly convinced, by the way, that you and I are somehow descended from Alexander and Marcus...

NICHOLAS

But...Alexander didn't have any children--did he--?

DR. OLIVER

Even if he didn't, we could still be descended from their family lines--uncles, aunts, cousins, whatever.

(pause)

Family traits carried down through the generations...bloodlines, genes persisting ...continuing down through the centuries ...spreading out over the entire globe...

(pause)

And here you and I are, exactly one thousand years later, the identical twins, according to Katrine, of Alexander and Marcus--

NICHOLAS

But--

DR. OLIVER holds up a hand. He's on a roll now.

DR. OLIVER

Imagine: Alexander and Marcus attempting to bring Katrine to the Holy Sanctuary. To awaken her from her coma--and to accomplish some other, much

larger purpose, which even they, like you and I, may not have clearly understood. Their destinies were inextricably bound up with hers...
(pause)
And then their ship went down. For them, everything came to a halt; all their destinies were...<u>interrupted</u>.
(pause)
I firmly believe in the power of destiny, Nicholas. And I've come to believe in the past short while that some destinies are so important that, if interrupted, <u>they cannot remain interrupted</u>.
(pause)
When Katrine's ship sank, the wheel of her destiny, Marcus's destiny, Alexander's destiny, suddenly ceased to turn. Now--after a period of exactly one thousand years--just as you and I are in the same city at the same time, probably for the first time in our lives, you--a <u>marine archeologist</u>, for the love of God!-- discover Katrine's casket.
(pause)
And the wheel of destiny abruptly jerks into motion once again.
(pause)
As though, the moment that the "stars" came into proper alignment again...<u>then, and only then</u>, could the sleeping princess be found...
(pause)
I firmly believe that Katrine must <u>complete</u> her interrupted journey to this Holy Sanctuary. It should have been with us. But now Ahrman has her...
(pause)
It's absolutely clear that Katrine has a powerful connection to the Sanctuary. <u>We</u> know it. <u>Ahrman</u> knows it now. We just don't know yet what this connection is.
(pause)
And if what Brother Antony said is true, Ahrman now has all four artifacts he needs to make up the <u>key</u> which will allow them to enter...

Both men are silent as the full weight of these words comes to rest on their shoulders. Suddenly, NICHOLAS slams his fist down on his knee.

NICHOLAS

We shouldn't be wasting all this time! We should be out there...<u>looking</u>...hunting down those <u>animals</u>...finding Pete and Katrine...
(pause)
They're counting on us, Cornelius...

DR. OLIVER

Going out blindly "hunting," as you put it, isn't going to do any good at all.
(pause)
If only I'd had a proper chance to look at the engraved scriptures on the tablet you found in Katrine's casket. I was so excited about bringing you here today that I didn't yet attempt to decipher them. And now Ahrman has the tablet--<u>and</u> the rubbings Sharon made of it...

A light of hope appears in NICHOLAS's eyes as a stunning realization hits him...

75 - <u>EXT. DESERTED FARMHOUSE - ESTABLISHING SHOT - NIGHT</u>

It's a rundown, abandoned building on the outskirts of the city. A parked vehicle is just visible behind it. Two of the four ZOMBIE OFFICERS are also visible, patrolling the outside of the house with their BAZOOKA weapons at the ready.

76 - <u>INT. DESERTED FARMHOUSE, KITCHEN - THAT MOMENT</u>

Sitting on the floor in the corner of the room, hands bound, mouth duct-taped, is PETER. ELSA stands watch near him. The other two ZOMBIE OFFICERS are guarding the two doors to the kitchen. KATRINE is seated on a straight-backed chair, her hands tied behind her. AHRMAN stands facing her.

KATRINE

H-How many different ways can I <u>tell</u> you? I don't know <u>where</u> this Holy Sanctuary is. I don't <u>know</u> if you can learn the--the secret of immortality there.

(beat)

And I especially don't know how <u>I</u> am connected to this place! I don't know what the birthmark on my hand means!

(beat)

I don't know anything!

AHRMAN stares speculatively at her.

AHRMAN

Perhaps if I were to...ask the <u>boy</u> some questions...it might loosen <u>your</u> tongue...

KATRINE explodes with sudden fury--

KATRINE

You--You are...<u>pathetic</u>! For years--For <u>years</u> I was told stories, <u>legends</u>, about the--the mighty Warlord Ahrman. <u>Mighty</u>--what a joke!

(beat)

Since the moment I first laid eyes on you, all I've seen you do is torture and threaten and do violence to those who are <u>weaker</u> than you, helpless, vulnerable...

(beat)

And now you threaten a child--

(beat)

What kind of man are you--?!

AHRMAN thrusts his hideous, rotting face into KATRINE's--

AHRMAN

I am the man who could kill you--<u>both of you</u>!--in the blink of an eye--Let us not forget that--!

KATRINE, trying not to cringe--

KATRINE

And let us not forget that you n-need me...alive--for whatever reason. You--

AHRMAN

(whirling away)

ENOUGH! There will be no more time wasted!

(beat)

Elsa! Bring the tablets and the orb to me!

ELSA leaps to his command, hands him the briefcase.

AHRMAN

(threateningly)

It does not <u>overly</u> concern me, <u>princess</u> ...that you will not answer my questions.

(pause)

One thousand years ago, I came very, very close to learning the answers <u>directly from the source</u>--

(holds the briefcase up)

Today, there will be <u>no</u> interruptions.

77 - <u>INT. MONASTERY, BROTHER ANTONY'S STUDY - NIGHT</u>

NICHOLAS and DR. OLIVER enter in an excited rush.

NICHOLAS

I don't know <u>why</u> I took the rubbings out of the briefcase! I wasn't thinking--I just did it when I was showing Brother Antony the tablet.

NICHOLAS's jacket is hanging on the back of a chair. His hand plunges into the pocket and emerges--holding the <u>TRACING PAPER RUBBINGS OF THE CRYSTAL TABLET THAT WAS FOUND WITH KATRINE IN HER CASKET</u>!

NICHOLAS

<u>Yes</u>!

(unfolds the pages)

God only knows what made me take them out of the briefcase...

DR. OLIVER

(smiling)

I'm sure you're exactly right: God knows very well what made you do it.

NICHOLAS gives him a startled look, a look that seems to say he's now been given some food for thought...

DR. OLIVER

(holding out his hand)

Now. Let's see what I can make of these inscriptions...

NICHOLAS hands him the TABLET RUBBINGS.

78 - <u>INT. DESERTED FARMHOUSE, KITCHEN - NIGHT</u>

AHRMAN's entire group is gathered now, including the two ZOMBIE OFFICERS who were previously patrolling the outside of the house.

AHRMAN

This time--<u>no interruptions</u>--

He gestures abruptly with his fists. Two BOLTS OF CRACKLING GREEN ENERGY hit the walls and vanish up through the ceiling.

79 - <u>EXT. DESERTED FARMHOUSE - THAT MOMENT</u>

The CRACKLING GREEN ENERGY emerges through the walls of the farmhouse. Within seconds, the entire building is <u>surrounded</u> by it, a magical, protective aura...

80 - <u>INT. MONASTERY, BROTHER ANTONY'S STUDY - NIGHT</u>

DR. OLIVER is hunched over the desk, examining the TABLET RUBBINGS with a magnifying glass and making notes.

DR. OLIVER

I think that's about... I think that's about all I can... There are a few gaps... but I think...yes, I think that's about all I can do...

NICHOLAS stops pacing the floor.

NICHOLAS

And--? What does it say--?

DR. OLIVER refers to his notepad, frowning.

DR. OLIVER

Well...
(pause)
First--the engraved scriptures confirm a great deal of what we learned from poor Brother Antony: The cleansing deluge that flooded the earth...the Ark coming to rest on a mountain-top...the divine creation of a Holy Sanctuary in the place where the Ark came to rest...an Eternal Guardian given some sort of physical form and left in this Sanctuary to watch over the earth, to maintain the cosmic balance between GOOD and EVIL...the unimaginable consequences for the world if this Sacred Sentinel were ever to be destroyed--

NICHOLAS

And does it say where this "Holy Sanctuary" is supposed to be?!

DR. OLIVER

Yes. Yes, it does. In a rather...cryptic fashion, actually...
(reads quote from notepad)
"...Near the far-eastern shores of the sea in the middle of the earth, seek the Trinity..."

NICHOLAS

The "Trinity"--?

DR. OLIVER pulls out a huge WORLD ATLAS from one of BROTHER ANTONY's bookshelves.

DR. OLIVER

(flipping pages)
..."the sea in the middle of the earth"... That can only mean--

NICHOLAS

--the Mediterranean--

DR. OLIVER

Yes... Yes...

DR. OLIVER finds the correct page.

NICHOLAS

..."far-eastern shores"... That could be anywhere: Egypt, Israel, Saudi Arabia, Syria--

DR. OLIVER

Or Turkey--

NICHOLAS

(sighs)
Which of course brings us back to Mount Ararat--

DR. OLIVER

Yes, but Mount Ararat is in eastern Turkey. More than 500 miles away from the shores of the Mediterranean.
(pause)
No... Not Mount Ararat...

(idea solidifying)

Yes... <u>Yes</u>...

NICHOLAS

<u>What</u>?

DR. OLIVER

(pointing to map)

These mountains here are known as the Taurus Mountains...

(pause)

<u>There</u>--I <u>thought</u> I recalled...

(taps map excitedly)

There is a grouping of three mountains that stand distinctly apart from the rest of the Taurus range.

(pause)

I'd completely forgotten this...but these three mountains are sometimes called--at least by the region's small Christian population--"The Father, Son, and the Holy Spirit"...

NICHOLAS

"The Father, Son, and the Holy Spirit"...

(pause)

The <u>Trinity</u>...!

(pause)

But...but which of the three mountains is the one we want...?

(pause)

Do the tablet inscriptions say anything else?

DR. OLIVER consults his note-pad again.

DR. OLIVER

"...Near the far-eastern shores of the sea in the middle of the earth, seek the Trinity..."

(finger moves down note-pad)

"...closest to God shall be the safest resting place..."

NICHOLAS

"Closest to God"...?

DR. OLIVER

Hmmm.

(pause)

In the mind of the ancients...the higher up you were, the closer you were to God...

NICHOLAS

Right! Church steeples, cathedral spires...

(pause)

Which means...

DR. OLIVER

"Closest to God" has got to mean the <u>tallest</u> of the three mountains!

(examines the map's elevation data)

Which means that...

(points)

<u>Yes</u>! It's got to be. The western-most mountain. The tallest of the three. The Holy Spirit...!

NICHOLAS

(wonderingly)

So...we've found our destination...

DR. OLIVER

Yes...

(pause)

And we'd better waste no time in making our way there, my friend.

(deadly serious)

The tablet scriptures categorically confirm that the three tablets and the orb, when attached to each other somehow, <u>do</u> serve as the only key to the Holy Sanctuary...

81 - <u>INT. DESERTED FARMHOUSE, KITCHEN - NIGHT</u>

AHRMAN and ELSA face each other across an old kitchen table. The room is hushed, expectant. AHRMAN removes the CRYSTAL ORB from the open briefcase and hands it to her.

AHRMAN

Two hands--<u>TWO</u> HANDS! Careful--!

Next, AHRMAN removes the THREE CRYSTAL TABLETS. Suddenly, the CRYSTAL ORB <u>begins to glow</u>. All at once--

AHRMAN

Yes!

--THREE SLOTS appear in the CRYSTAL ORB's previously smooth exterior. At the same moment, from outside: an ANGRY RUMBLE OF THUNDER. AHRMAN glances up and smiles. KATRINE and PETER look up, afraid. As ELSA continues to hold the ORB, AHRMAN inserts the points of the three TRIANGULAR TABLETS into the THREE SLOTS. By the third insertion, the ORB's glow has become blinding--and the ORB itself is shuddering and vibrating in ELSA's hands. Startled, she almost drops it--

AHRMAN

Release it.

ELSA obeys. The ORB, with the INSERTED TABLETS, floats. Its brilliant light fills the whole kitchen. The SOUND OF THUNDER shakes the walls of the house--THUNDER, followed by the SOUL-WRENCHING CRASH of a <u>BOLT OF LIGHTNING</u>--

82 - <u>EXT. DESERTED FARMHOUSE - THAT MOMENT</u>

The BOLT OF LIGHTNING strikes the roof--but, amazingly, it bounces off and FIZZLES out harmlessly in the air. As does a SECOND BOLT. And a THIRD. And a FOURTH. The CRACKLING GREEN ENERGY AURA is serving its purpose...

83 - <u>INT. DESERTED FARMHOUSE, KITCHEN - THAT MOMENT</u>

AHRMAN listens to the violent but futile SOUNDS OF THE STORM, smiling. The ORB--with its PROTRUDING TABLETS--is still floating in mid-air. All at once, it starts to <u>rotate</u>, slowly at first, then faster, and faster--and the brilliant light pulses, on and off, on and off--

--SUDDENLY!--although ALL THE PEOPLE in the room remain IN FOCUS, everything else <u>starts to change</u>: Background objects lose their sharpness, become blurry, hazy, colors shifting, smudging. The entire farmhouse kitchen seems to be <u>physically transforming</u> around them--

DISSOLVE TO:

84 - <u>EXT. MOUNTAIN, NORTH-WEST FACE, SUMMIT - MORNING</u>

--and just as suddenly, the background begins to regain its sharpness, the hazy blur focuses, the smudged colors separate and take on startling clarity. <u>And that's the moment we realize that it isn't a transformation that has taken place, it's a transportation</u>. The group is no longer in a farmhouse kitchen, <u>they are at the mist-wreathed summit of a mountain</u>! It's a snow-covered plateau on which they find themselves, a shelf that juts from the base of a smooth vertical wall of solid rock. PETER is sitting on the snow, his hands still bound and his mouth still duct-taped. KATRINE still sits on the straight-backed chair, her hands tied behind her. AHRMAN, ELSA, and the four ZOMBIE OFFICERS stand nearby. The pulsating ORB--with its PROTRUDING TABLETS--is still floating in mid-air. But it's no longer rotating; now, it seems to be <u>waiting</u>...

AHRMAN approaches KATRINE.

AHRMAN

Do you see--<u>princess</u>--my orb and my tablets have brought us here to our final destination!

AHRMAN tears the bonds from KATRINE's wrists and she stands.

KATRINE

So you're finally going to get what you want. No matter at what cost to mankind.

Although there is triumph in AHRMAN's eyes, he seems tired, weaker. The decay of his physical form is progressing rapidly.

AHRMAN

So you perceived it, then? The knowledge, the understanding...it flooded you, just as it did me, during the transportation...

KATRINE

Yes.

AHRMAN

(grinning exultantly)
And whosoever shall kill the Sacred Sentinel and consume its blood shall steal its ultimate power, <u>steal its eternal life</u>, steal its--

KATRINE utters a gasp of revulsion and steps back. AHRMAN's decaying right ear has just dropped off. AHRMAN looks at it, lying in the snow. The sight sobers him.

KATRINE

(slowly realizing)
The decay...it's caused by your sorcery, isn't it? Every time you use your sorcery, your body rots a little more...

AHRMAN ignores her. He's made an abrupt decision. He strides to PETER, rips off his bonds, tears away the duct tape. Then he seizes PETER's wrist and yanks him, struggling, to his feet.

AHRMAN

Then perhaps it's time I found myself a new body to reside in...!

Before KATRINE can react, AHRMAN's eyes are blazing with green fire--which suddenly extinguishes. Instantly, the green energy begins to crackle where AHRMAN's hand is gripping PETER's wrist. But just as suddenly, this fizzles out, and the green light returns to AHRMAN's eyes.

AHRMAN

No!

AHRMAN tries again, his face twisted into a grimace of immense effort. But this time, the green light doesn't even leave his eyes. He can't do it. He cannot transfer his life-force any more. He is trapped inside the body he's now inhabiting. His teeth bared in a snarl of panic and rage, AHRMAN flings PETER aside. KATRINE rushes to the boy's side.

AHRMAN hurls a blast of energy at KATRINE and PETER. Before they can move, the green light surrounds them, magically creating a cage-like box with the two of them inside.

KATRINE

What are you doing?!

AHRMAN turns his back on them. ELSA and the four ZOMBIE OFFICERS, armed with their BAZOOKA weapons, surround the box.

AHRMAN

Ensuring you don't get any notions about trying to escape.
(pause)
If I must bide my time in this body until eternal life is finally mine...

(pause)

...then I will do so with my sorcerous powers at <u>full strength</u>...

AHRMAN crosses his legs and closes his eyes--<u>levitating two feet off the ground</u>. Tendrils of crackling energy surround him, spiraling towards his body, <u>feeding</u> him, <u>recharging</u> him...

85 - <u>EXT. TOWN OF ERTA, TURKEY, MARKETPLACE - DUSK</u>

The marketplace is still busy, even as the day draws to a close. With a cell-phone to his ear, DR. OLIVER is leaning in the open back door of a rented jeep. RONIM, sitting on the front seat, watches as DR. OLIVER tucks a tarpaulin over <u>a pile of weapons</u> on the back seat. At the other side of the market is a TELEVISION VAN, complete with a small satellite transmitter/receiver dish on its roof. On the VAN's side is the logo of the "GLOBAL BROADCASTING NETWORK." NICHOLAS approaches DR. OLIVER, having just finished talking to the occupants of the VAN.

                    DR. OLIVER
(into the phone)
I-I've got to go.
(pause, listens)
I...I love you too. I mean that.
(pause)
'Bye...

DR. OLIVER snaps the phone shut, aware that NICHOLAS is looking at him curiously.

                    DR. OLIVER
Just...talking to my wife. Back home.
(pause)
We haven't been getting on very well, you see. Not for quite a while.

(pause)

It just seemed really important that I speak to her now. Before we...you know...

(swipes at his eyes)

But enough of that. Tell me--<u>were you successful</u>?

NICHOLAS looks excited.

NICHOLAS

The most amazing luck! It's a TV film crew, making a documentary about the world's lesser-known mountain ranges--and they've been renting an <u>army helicopter</u> to use for aerial filming!

(pause)

They're willing to rent <u>us</u> the helicopter! As well as their pilot!

(pause)

Unbelievable coincidence...!

DR. OLIVER

(smiling)

Rather than "luck" or "coincidence"... don't you think it's more appropriate to call it "fate"? You must see that now, don't you?

NICHOLAS hesitates--then finally nods. He turns to stare at the jagged peaks of the Taurus mountain range, clearly visible in the background.

NICHOLAS

Cornelius...what do you think is <u>really</u> happening here?

(pause)

Are we here to prevent some sort of... turn of-the-millennium Armageddon?

DR. OLIVER

(sighs)

I don't know. I honestly don't know.

(pause)

But I <u>think</u> the answer is <u>yes</u>...

86 - <u>EXT. MOUNTAIN, NORTH-WEST FACE, SUMMIT - MORNING</u>

KATRINE and PETER are still trapped in AHRMAN's magical box-like prison. They are sitting on the ground holding on to each other. Not for warmth--the box has kept out the cold--but for comfort.

PETER

D'you think, when this is all over...d'you think you'll stay with us...live with us, I mean...?

KATRINE

Pete--I don't know.

PETER

My Uncle Nick. He really...I think he really needs you in his life...

KATRINE

It's so strange.
(pause)
But I think I need him too...

AHRMAN (O.S.)

I am choked with emotion.

KATRINE and PETER jump to their feet, turn around. AHRMAN is standing outside the prison. Although still rotting, his body once again looks immensely powerful and energized.

AHRMAN

But I wouldn't be making any long-term plans for the future, if I were you.

KATRINE

How long are you planning to keep us in here?! The boy is <u>starving</u>--

                              AHRMAN

Shut up.

*With a wave of his hand, the magical prison vanishes. The ZOMBIE OFFICERS herd
KATRINE and PETER over to the smooth vertical wall of solid rock where the
pulsating ORB--with its PROTRUDING TABLETS--is still floating in mid-air,
still* waiting.

                              AHRMAN

Now.

Suddenly, a narrow beam of pure light shoots out from the ORB *and strikes the
rock wall.*

                              AHRMAN

Yes! YES--!!

An oval-shaped expanse of the rock wall begins to ripple, *loses density, then
vanishes. It flickers back, vanishes, flickers back, vanishes, flickers back-
-then vanishes, this time for good. What remains is a large OVAL PORTAL.
AHRMAN turns to KATRINE with a fearsome, eager smile.*

                              AHRMAN

After you...

87 - <u>INT. MOUNTAIN, TUNNEL - MORNING</u>

*The tunnel beyond the OVAL PORTAL is narrow, winding, with a number of
branching-off side tunnels. Following AHRMAN's directions, they make their
way: KATRINE in the lead, AHRMAN right behind her, ushering her along; then
ELSA, PETER and the four ZOMBIE OFFICERS. Suddenly: a glimmer of blue-green
light coming from around a turn in the tunnel up ahead--*

KATRINE is the first to make the turn. She comes to a jerking stop, her mouth dropping open, the strange light playing across her face...

88 - EXT. MOUNTAIN - ESTABLISHING SHOT - MORNING

The western-most mountain of the grouping known as "The Trinity" looms against the sky. Clouds partially obscure the summit--at an altitude of close to 15,000 feet. A rugged-looking ARMY HELICOPTER is hovering there amidst the clouds. A cable has been lowered to the mountain peak...

89 - EXT. MOUNTAIN, NORTH-WEST FACE, SUMMIT - MORNING

Next to a hold-all containing their weapons, NICHOLAS stands on the snow-covered plateau looking up. DR. OLIVER, in a harness--with RONIM strapped to his body--is being lowered by cable from the HELICOPTER. Once they're safely down, NICHOLAS helps him and RONIM out of the harness. He then waves the HELICOPTER away. The sound of its whirling blades dwindles as it leaves them.

DR. OLIVER

I-I've never been so glad to be on solid ground in all my life!
(pause)
Are you <u>sure</u> this is the correct place?

Without saying a word, NICHOLAS points over DR. OLIVER's shoulder. The older man turns.

DR. OLIVER

Oh...<u>my</u>...

The CRYSTAL ORB is still emitting its beam of light at the vertical rock wall. The OVAL PORTAL still yawns--

NICHOLAS

Oh...<u>shit</u>--

The OVAL PORTAL has begun to flicker in and out of existence--

90 - <u>INT. MOUNTAIN, TUNNEL/CAVERN - MORNING</u>

KATRINE's stupefied expression is duplicated on PETER's face. AHRMAN merely looks <u>triumphant</u>. Just beyond this final turn, the tunnel opens up into an impossibly immense CAVERN, its floor shaped like the bottom of a colossal bowl, a turbulent sea of rock and ice, frozen solid. A smooth, concave sheet of ice curves down to the cave floor, where hundreds of stalagmites thrust up. The ceiling of the cavern is a great glacial canopy of ice through which daylight filters and from which hundreds of stalactites hang. As overwhelming as this cavern is, however, attention is primarily focused on one particular place within it: a spot near the opposite wall... For there, jammed into a crevice of ice, is <u>NOAH's ARK</u>. The ARK is a huge, wooden, barge-like vessel, boxy, rough-hewn. <u>We are actually looking at NOAH's ARK, preserved in this cave for untold thousands of years</u>...!

                         PETER

Wow... <u>Wow</u>...

                         AHRMAN

We go down--<u>now</u>.

                          ELSA

But--how--?

                         AHRMAN

Like...<u>this</u>--

Before KATRINE can react, AHRMAN reaches behind him, seizes PETER's arm, yanks him forward, and pushes him over the edge.

                         KATRINE

No-oo--!!

On his back, feet first, PETER slides down the smooth sweep of ice--

PETER

Whooo-ooo-ooaaahhh--!!!

--down the icy slide he goes...down...and finally comes to a spinning stop next to a cluster of stalagmites.

KATRINE

Peter--are you all right--?! Are you all right--!!? Peter--!!

Dazed, PETER struggles to a sitting position.

PETER

Y-Yeah...Yeah...I'm fine...! I'm okay!

As he's getting to his feet, PETER snaps off a long, thin stalagmite and conceals it in the sleeve of his shirt...

AHRMAN grips KATRINE's arm and together they descend slowly, levitated magically down through the air--leaving ELSA and the four ZOMBIE OFFICERS up at the tunnel opening.

ELSA

What about us?!

Halfway down to the cavern floor, AHRMAN bellows back:

AHRMAN

You saw the boy! DO IT!

AHRMAN's and KATRINE's feet touch the ground. KATRINE immediately shrugs free of his grip.

PETER (O.S.)

Oh wow... Oh...<u>wow</u>...

PETER has moved closer to the ARK--but his eyes are now fixed on something else. AHRMAN and KATRINE approach him. (In the background, ELSA slides down the slope of ice as the ZOMBIE OFFICERS wait their turn.) KATRINE places her hands on PETER's shoulders.

KATRINE

You're sure you're not hur--?

She GASPS, seeing what it is that PETER is staring at: Beside the ARK is a raised granite PLATFORM surrounded by an AURA OF INTENSE WHITE RADIANCE. Within the light is an OLIVE TREE--the tree of <u>peace</u>. <u>Perched on one of the branches is a DOVE</u>. The bird cocks its head, staring at KATRINE, wise, knowing.

AHRMAN

The...Sentinel...

KATRINE is overwhelmed with unexpected emotion, her eyes shining with tears. ELSA and the four ZOMBIE OFFICERS, all on the cavern floor now, join the others. AHRMAN steps closer to the raised PLATFORM, then stops. He turns instead to the closest ZOMBIE OFFICER.

AHRMAN

You! Bring me the dove...

KATRINE

No!

But the chosen OFFICER has already set down his BAZOOKA and is mounting the flight of rocky steps that lead up to the PLATFORM. He moves into the white radiance--<u>and bursts into flame</u>. He stumbles backwards, enveloped in holy white fire. Because he is already dead, his screams are <u>silent</u>, chilling.

Within seconds, his charred body is a motionless heap on the icy cavern floor, sending up plumes of smoke and steam.

AHRMAN's eyes ignite with sudden realization. He grips KATRINE's arm.

                              AHRMAN
You--it's you--!!

KATRINE stares at him uncomprehendingly.

                              AHRMAN
You are the one who must go into the light and bring the dove out to me. It is you who will enable me to achieve eternal life! That is your purpose--!

                              KATRINE
No. No. I won't do it.

AHRMAN's face darkens with anger.

                              KATRINE
You cannot do this! The fate of mankind--!

AHRMAN yanks PETER viciously towards him--

                              AHRMAN
Defy me--princess--and I send the boy in.

91 - EXT. MOUNTAIN, NORTH-WEST FACE, SUMMIT - MORNING

NICHOLAS, DR. OLIVER and RONIM stand by the rock wall. The OVAL PORTAL is still flickering in and out of existence.

                              DR. OLIVER
Approximately every 1.7 seconds, the hole disappears. It returns again after 2.3 seconds or thereabouts--

NICHOLAS

We've got to time this just right. You and Ronim had better go first.

DR. OLIVER nods nervously.

DR. OLIVER

(to Ronim)

Jump with me--okay, boy--?

DR. OLIVER and RONIM time their jump perfectly and make it safely through just before the PORTAL flickers out of existence again. NICHOLAS times his jump just as perfectly--and makes it

92 - INT. MOUNTAIN, TUNNEL - THAT MOMENT

Through!--just before the PORTAL vanishes, this time apparently for good, for it doesn't appear again...

NICHOLAS

Let's go--

93 - INT. CAVERN - MORNING

KATRINE makes her way hesitantly up the steps that lead to the granite platform. ELSA has her arm locked around PETER's throat, the barrel of a hand-gun jammed against his temple. Close by are the three remaining ZOMBIE OFFICERS, their BAZOOKA weapons at the ready. AHRMAN, his decayed face glowing with anticipation, holds a knife--a knife with which he intends to sacrifice the Holy Sentinel, before consuming the sacred blood that will give him ultimate power and eternal life... KATRINE stops on the final stair before the platform, paralyzed, trembling.

Sixty feet up the side of the cavern, NICHOLAS, DR. OLIVER and RONIM peer down over a rocky ledge. They are amazed...

NICHOLAS

My God... My...<u>God</u>...

<u>ANGLE ON</u> *KATRINE: paralyzed, trembling.*

AHRMAN (O.S.)

I am <u>waiting</u>--<u>PRINCESS</u>--!!

With a lurch, KATRINE steps up onto the platform...<u>and enters the holy aura</u>.
Nothing happens to her. She continues to move forward, unscathed. The OLIVE
TREE is vibrant with rich life. The DOVE is blamelessly white and pure. Its
wise eyes watch as KATRINE approaches; in them, the light of <u>recognition</u>...
KATRINE's face is flushed with happiness now, her eyes brimming with joyful
tears. She comes to stand below the perched DOVE. She reaches up and the
trusting bird hops from its branch into her cupped palms.

Instantly, the holy aura surrounding the OLIVE TREE fades, then vanishes
completely. Her joy also fading, KATRINE turns slowly to face AHRMAN.

AHRMAN

(hungrily)
Bring the Sentinel...to me...

KATRINE steps down off the platform--but freezes on the first stair. AHRMAN
moves swiftly to the foot of the steps, thrusts out his hand.

AHRMAN

<u>Give...it...to me</u>...

KATRINE looks about her helplessly. SHE CANNOT DO THIS! Suddenly, movement
across the cave catches her eye: she sees NICHOLAS and DR. OLIVER! NICHOLAS
is waving something at her--<u>an ARCHER's BOW</u>! She doesn't visibly react,
instead, she steps down two more stairs. AHRMAN steps up one.

AHRMAN

GIVE IT TO ME...!

On the ledge, NICHOLAS is now also holding a QUIVER FULL OF ARROWS--and a
POLICE FORCE BAZOOKA. DR. OLIVER has the same weapon. NICHOLAS is seated, his
legs dangling over the icy slide.

AHRMAN

NOW--!!

KATRINE goes down one more step. She looks AHRMAN dead in the eye--then throws
the DOVE up into the air, out of his reach--at the same instant that NICHOLAS
launches himself down the icy slide--

KATRINE

(to Ahrman)
May your soul rot in Hell--

--KATRINE punches AHRMAN squarely in the mouth. He is knocked backwards off
the step and stumbles into the path of NICHOLAS, rocketing down the icy slide.
NICHOLAS WHACKS AHRMAN in the back of the knees with the butt of his BAZOOKA,
sending the WARLORD sprawling. As NICHOLAS slides to a stop, we see DR. OLIVER
in the background about to launch from the ledge. NICHOLAS throws the BOW and
QUIVER FULL OF ARROWS to KATRINE, who deftly catches them. In the space of a
second, she has the strap of the quiver over her shoulder and an arrow slapped
into position against the bow. She swings around to face ELSA and takes aim-
-

--ELSA jams the gun-barrel against PETER's temple, her finger tightening on
the trigger. But at the same instant, KATRINE lets the arrow fly. It slams
into the tiny space inside ELSA's gun's trigger-guard, behind the trigger--
preventing the trigger from moving--before piercing ELSA's shoulder. With a
cry of pain, ELSA flinches back--

KATRINE

Pete--! <u>RUN</u>--!!

PETER twists free of ELSA'S grip and stumbles towards KATRINE on the steps. AHRMAN, meanwhile, is on his feet again--but only for a second--for that's when DR. OLIVER <u>whizzes down the ice slide</u>--

DR. OLIVER

Whoo-<u>HOOOOOOOO</u>--!!!

--knocking AHRMAN's legs out from under him again--

KATRINE helps PETER up the steps to the shelter of the OLIVE TREE.

KATRINE

(quickly)
Are you all right--?

PETER nods shakily--and suddenly NICHOLAS is there, his arms tightly around both of them. Abruptly, BAZOOKA-fire--from OFFICERS 1 and 3 hits the tree, above them. KATRINE, NICHOLAS and PETER jump for cover off the side of the platform.

<u>ANGLE ON</u> ELSA: The shock of being hit by KATRINE's arrow has literally <u>knocked her free of AHRMAN's hypnotic control</u>. The red is gone from her eyes-- permanently. Weeping, gritting her teeth, she pulls the arrow out of her shoulder.

ELSA

Oh God...What have I done WHAT HAVE I <u>DONE</u>--?!!

Free of AHRMAN's trance, ELSA is filled with the desire for <u>revenge</u> against him. She picks up the BAZOOKA left behind by the ZOMBIE OFFICER who burned to a crisp in the holy light...

NICHOLAS, KATRINE and PETER are taking cover in the avenue between the ARK and the granite platform. DR. OLIVER is desperate to make a dash to join them, but OFFICER 2's BAZOOKA-fire has him trapped behind a cluster of boulders.

ELSA, tears streaming, has made her way to AHRMAN. She raises the BAZOOKA.

ELSA

What you made me <u>do</u>...!

AHRMAN, seething with madness and fury, sends an energy blast hurtling at ELSA. She barely manages to dive for cover. The blast explodes against the ice-rock floor, cracking it, creating a deep, deep fissure that grows ever deeper. AHRMAN strides towards her hiding-place. She sees him coming and tries to run--but not quickly enough. With a sorcerous wave of his hand, he sends her flying. She lands with a terrible THUD, rolls, slides--<u>and slips into the now-bottomless fissure in the ice-rock floor</u>. At the last second, she manages to grip the edge of the crack and clings on for her life.

AHRMAN, believing ELSA disposed of, sets off in pursuit of the DOVE. KATRINE, having seen what just occurred, rushes towards ELSA, dodging BAZOOKA-fire.

NICHOLAS

Katrine--NO!!

KATRINE reaches ELSA.

KATRINE

Give me your hand!

ELSA grips KATRINE's hand with her right hand--but the left one suddenly slips. <u>She is dangling in the crevice with her life literally in KATRINE's hand</u>.

ELSA

I can't--I CAN'T--!!

KATRINE

Hold on! Don't let go--!!

ELSA

Please...forgive me for what I've done... It wasn't me...

KATRINE

We know that. Just hold on--NICHOLAS--!!

ELSA

Promise me...you'll tell my family...I love--

ELSA's hand slips from KATRINE's and she plummets into the bottomless crevice to her death. KATRINE backs away from the edge, stunned.

ANGLE ON DR. OLIVER, cornered by OFFICER 2's BAZOOKA-fire. Suddenly, OFFICER 2 is distracted by the DOVE flying over his head. DR. OLIVER takes his chance, bobs up from behind a boulder, and fires his BAZOOKA. OFFICER 2's head is blown to bits. OFFICER 1, seeing what has happened to his fellow ZOMBIE, charges at DR. OLIVER.

Meanwhile, NICHOLAS has helped KATRINE return to the relative safety of their hiding-place beside the ARK.

NICHOLAS
(to Katrine and Peter)
I'll get Cornelius. We have to find a way out of here--fast--

KATRINE

What about the Sentinel--?

Suddenly--

DR. OLIVER (O.S.)

NICHOLA--!!

His cry is lost in a CHOKED GURGLE.

NICHOLAS

Wait here--

KATRINE

(grips his arm)

<u>I'll</u> help Dr. Oliver...

KATRINE points to a spot some fifty feet away. The DOVE is now perched on a ledge halfway up the cavern wall. <u>And AHRMAN is below the ledge, quietly levitating up through the air</u>...

KATRINE (CONT'D)

...unless you want to trade weapons with me...?

DR. OLIVER is on his back. OFFICER 1 straddles him, choking him.

<u>ANGLE ON</u> AHRMAN, rising stealthily up, up...

<u>ANGLE ON</u> KATRINE: She is now crouched behind a boulder, desperately trying to get to DR. OLIVER. OFFICER 3's BAZOOKA-fire is forcing her to keep her head down. She has an arrow in position on her bow, but she can't hit DR. OLIVER's attacker from her position. <u>She gets an idea</u>: high above DR. OLIVER and his attacker, there hangs a cluster of STALACTITES. KATRINE takes aim at these STALACTITES. <u>FIRES</u>. The arrow strikes one of the STALACTITES about halfway along its length, <u>breaking it</u>--

--<u>ANGLE ON</u> DR. OLIVER's PURPLE FACE, mouth gasping, as OFFICER 1's hands <u>squeeze</u>. DR. OLIVER sees the broken STALACTITE plummet, strike his attacker in the back of the head and <u>burst</u> out of his forehead--

--<u>ANGLE ON</u> AHRMAN: He is about to seize the DOVE--

NICHOLAS (O.S.)

DON'T TOUCH IT, FREAK--

Hovering by the ledge, AHRMAN looks down. Directly below him, NICHOLAS is crouched--with his BAZOOKA pointed straight up between AHRMAN's slightly parted legs--

NICHOLAS

I hope you're not planning to have any little baby warlocks--

NICHOLAS fires the BAZOOKA. The blast rockets upwards. AHRMAN instinctively jerks his feet together--with the result that the blast <u>drives up</u> against the soles of his boots and he, in turn, is driven upwards by the impact. He CRASHES into the cavern's glacier-roof, spins, and starts hurling BLASTS of deadly energy down at NICHOLAS.

NICHOLAS dives for cover--<u>but then abruptly the blasts stop</u>. The DOVE has flown from its perch and AHRMAN is now trying a different approach to getting hold of it. He SLAPS his palms together and a BEAM OF RED LIGHT shoots from his hands across the cavern, <u>and envelops the DOVE in mid-air</u>. Although the DOVE's wings are flapping furiously, it is no longer flying forwards: now, it is moving <u>backwards</u>...<u>towards AHRMAN</u>. As he reels the bird in along the beam of red light, AHRMAN slowly levitates himself down through the air. The moment his boots touch the ground--that's the same moment he closes his rotting hands around the SACRED SENTINEL's immaculate body--

--<u>AND THAT'S WHEN THE TREMORS BEGIN</u>: First, there's just a RUMBLING SOUND, getting louder by the second, but within moments, <u>the entire cavern is quaking</u>. The cavern floor shudders. Clumps of ice break from the ceiling, rocks bouncing down the walls. OFFICER 3 is knocked to the ground and KATRINE seizes the opportunity: she runs/stumbles over to DR. OLIVER. He is sitting up, massaging his throat.

KATRINE

Are you all right--?

DR. OLIVER

Y-Yes... What's happening...?

KATRINE

I don't know--
(*takes his arm*)
Come on--we have to get back to Nicholas and Peter--

DR. OLIVER

(*sincerely*)
Thank you, my dear. Thank you.

KATRINE grins at him, helps him to his feet--

ANGLE ON NICHOLAS, returning to the ARK across the heaving cavern floor.

PETER

U-Uncle Nick--!?

KATRINE and DR. OLIVER stumble up to them.

KATRINE

What is it? What's causing this?!

NICHOLAS

The second that Ahrman touched the dove--that's when the tremors started: the exact second--

DR. OLIVER

Almost as if he caused some kind of violent disruption in the cosmic equilibrium--

KATRINE

But where is he n--OhmyGOD--

AHRMAN is across the cavern, one hand clamped around the DOVE, the other gripping his KNIFE.

NICHOLAS points his BAZOOKA at AHRMAN. Suddenly, he sees, off to his right, OFFICER 3 about to shoot his weapon at their group. NICHOLAS swings his BAZOOKA around and <u>fires</u>. A gaping hole appears in the dead center of OFFICER 3's chest. NICHOLAS swings his BAZOOKA back towards AHRMAN--as the crazed WARLORD raises his knife to the DOVE's throat. NICHOLAS prepares to fire--

KATRINE

Wait--! Are you sure you can hit Ahrman without hitting the dove--?!

NICHOLAS

Of <u>course</u>--

KATRINE

(urgently)
That man you just shot--what part of his body were you aiming at--?

NICHOLAS

Er...His head...

Without another word, NICHOLAS gives KATRINE the BAZOOKA. Swiftly, confidently, she aims--<u>and fires</u>. The shot is perfect, blasting the knife from AHRMAN's grip, making him jerk back and <u>lose hold of the DOVE</u>. The blast continues and explodes into the cave wall.

AHRMAN

(beyond insanity now)
NOOOOOO--!!!!

But his cry is cut off as an <u>avalanche</u> of ROCKS and ICE CHUNKS comes CRASHING down on top of him--and the <u>SACRED SENTINEL</u> once again escapes to safety--

PETER

Uncle Nick--I...I...think we'd better get out of here--<u>NOW</u>--

The ENTIRE CAVERN FLOOR is heaving, cracking, grinding, breaking apart as the tremors intensify. Even worse--<u>the cavern is beginning to flood</u>, melting ice water pouring in from great fissures appearing in the ice and rock. The glacial roof fractures and shifts with an OMINOUS CREAKING, sending stalactites arrowing down.

KATRINE

There's only one place we might be safe--!
(beat)
<u>On the Ark</u>--!

94 - <u>EXT. TOWN OF ERTA, OUTSKIRTS - MORNING</u>

Near a scattering of huts is parked the "GLOBAL BROADCASTING NETWORK" TELEVISION VAN, with the Taurus mountain range <u>very near in the background</u>. The TV film crew is in the process of packing up equipment.

CAMERAMAN

(to his assistant)
What the <u>hell</u>...?

<u>ANGLE ON</u> THE WESTERN-MOST MOUNTAIN of the grouping of three known as "The Trinity." At the summit, snow is pluming up in clouds. And suddenly audible: <u>a distant, threatening RUMBLE</u>...

95 - <u>INT. MOUNTAIN SUMMIT, CAVERN - MORNING</u>

<u>ANGLE ON</u> THE DECK OF THE ARK: KATRINE and PETER have already climbed on board using ropes that NICHOLAS and DR. OLIVER had brought with them. Around them, the cavern is in chaos: water flooding in from a hundred places; ice and rock melting, shifting, the sound DEAFENING. The glacial ceiling is CRACKING, CREAKING. <u>And the ARK is slowly breaking free from its crevice of ice</u>...

PETER

What's taking them so long?!

KATRINE

I don't--<u>wait</u>--here they are, thank God!

KATRINE and PETER haul DR. OLIVER and NICHOLAS over the rail and onto the deck. NICHOLAS is holding RONIM securely under one arm.

DR. OLIVER

I think the poor little fellow froze his bottom sliding down that ice-slide...

RONIM whimpers as if to say, "And that's not all I froze!"

95 - <u>EXT. BOTTOM OF MOUNTAIN - MORNING</u>

The "GLOBAL BROADCASTING NETWORK" TELEVISION VAN has sped the short distance to the bottom of the western-most mountain of "The Trinity." So have crowds of ERTA TOWNSPEOPLE. The film crew is hurriedly setting up equipment. On the VAN roof, the small satellite dish is rotating to a new position.

TECHNICIAN

(to cameraman)
Two minutes! We'll be live on the air in two minutes--!

96 - <u>INT. MOUNTAIN SUMMIT, CAVERN - MORNING</u>

The ARK has almost completely broken free from its crevice of ice. Flooding water surges around it.

NICHOLAS

We'll have to go below deck--and just hope the Ark will be enough protection until this subsides--!

Suddenly, the ARK wrenches completely free from its ice mooring. It pitches and tips and rocks in the rising waters.

DR. OLIVER

Oh--my <u>God</u>...

They all look up. The cavern's immense ice roof is CREAKING HORRENDOUSLY, about to collapse on top of them--

NICHOLAS

Everyone below deck--now!

With a TUMULTUOUS ROAR, <u>one whole side of the cavern</u> suddenly crumbles away. Through the gaping hole that results, <u>blinding daylight</u> pours--and immediately the rushing water starts to channel towards the opening. The ARK, caught in the powerful current, is swung around--just as one side of the glacial ceiling swings part-way down. The flood waters rush towards the opening, taking with them ice floes and debris <u>and the ARK</u>. The gushing water bursts from the open side of the cavern like a waterfall, channeling the ancient ARK <u>out of the cavern</u>, just as the glacial ceiling CRASHES down with a SPLASHING <u>BOOM</u> behind them--

97 - <u>EXT. MOUNTAIN SUMMIT - MORNING</u>

On the deck of the ARK: the reluctant passengers are clinging to the ropes-- and to each other--<u>terrified</u>. The front of the vessel <u>DIPS DOWN</u> as it passes fully through the opening. Carried on a torrent of water, melting ice and loose debris, the ARK <u>begins to slide down the side of the mountain</u>. Surrounding the vessel is a <u>white, glowing aura</u>...

KATRINE

We have to get inside! The hatchway is--
(eyes widen)
No. <u>No</u>...

Set in the side of the box-like CABIN AREA in the center of the deck is the hatchway that leads below. Levitating magically up through this hatchway is the WARLORD AHRMAN. The decay of his body and face has progressed wildly; he is monstrously angry, monstrously insane.

AHRMAN

It...has...always been <u>you</u>, princess. For one thousand years...it has been <u>you</u>.
(beat)
Always in the <u>way</u>. Always <u>IN THE WAY</u>!!

AHRMAN glides towards KATRINE, unaffected by the ARK's slanted, JARRING, BOUNCING motion. He seizes her, begins hammering at her with his huge fists, forcing her down the inclined deck towards the bow.

NICHOLAS

<u>KATRINE</u>--!!

NICHOLAS, DR. OLIVER and PETER, clinging to the rail, go after them. The constant wind pushes them back. AHRMAN bashes KATRINE, sending her SLAMMING into the rail at the bow. For a sickening second, she is balanced on her back on the rail. Below her, the mountainside flashes by under the ARK's hull. <u>And then AHRMAN leaps on her</u>. His hands clamp around her throat--

98 - <u>EXT. BOTTOM OF MOUNTAIN - MORNING</u>

TECHNICIAN

Are you getting this?! Are you getting this?!
CAMERAMAN

Yeah...uh...<u>yeah</u>...

ANGLE ON A NEARBY TV MONITOR: On the screen, the mountain is visible; a DARK SHAPE rushes down over the snow-covered slopes. Below this image are the words: "LIVE FEED - WORLDWIDE"...

99 - <u>EXT. ARK, DECK - THAT MOMENT</u>

NICHOLAS and DR. OLIVER are bracing themselves against the rail, trying to get a clear BAZOOKA-shot at AHRMAN. The ARK continues to speed down the mountainside, BOUNCING, SHUDDERING, carrying with it a great tide of rocky debris, melting ice and snow--and it is obvious <u>that this should not be possible</u>, and yet, <u>surrounded by its glowing white aura</u>, the ARK barrels onwards, defying the laws of nature...

NICHOLAS
We can't shoot from here--! We might hit Katrine--!

NICHOLAS charges at AHRMAN, only to be knocked aside. He falls to the deck, stunned. PETER, meanwhile, is moving along the rail towards throttling AHRMAN and struggling with KATRINE. He's withdrawing something from the sleeve of his shirt: <u>it's the long, thin stalagmite he took from the cavern</u>.

KATRINE manages to struggle loose and lunges away from AHRMAN. DR. OLIVER jumps at the opportunity and fires the BAZOOKA. But he isn't fast enough: AHRMAN dives at KATRINE and the BAZOOKA-BLAST sails uselessly over his shoulder. KATRINE is dragged back to the rail. And AHRMAN's hands once again encircle her throat--

Suddenly, the hurtling ARK is <u>VIOLENTLY JOLTED</u> by something in its path. PETER stumbles and rolls down the inclined deck. He hits the bulwark to the left of AHRMAN and KATRINE, breaking his ankle. NICHOLAS is on his feet again and leaps on AHRMAN's back--but before he can get a firm hold on the WARLORD's neck, AHRMAN bucks, thrashes and flings him off.

KATRINE's HAND is clawing in spasms at the rail. She is almost unconscious. PETER, unable to stand, presses the stalagmite into her palm. She lifts her hand and sees what she's been given--just as NICHOLAS leaps again, this time slamming AHRMAN sideways. With AHRMAN's grip loosened, <u>KATRINE thrusts the</u>

stalagmite upwards, into his throat, through his tongue, into the roof of his mouth, into his brain. His hands loosen and KATRINE wrenches free, gasping--

NICHOLAS

(aiming BAZOOKA)

Cornelius--NOW--!!

DR. OLIVER and NICHOLAS both fire at the same time at AHRMAN, who is turning around, staggering. The blasts knock him back against the rail at the bow. DR. OLIVER and NICHOLAS prepare to fire again. But before they can--from off to the side, KATRINE dives low, seizes AHRMAN just below the knees, pulls up his legs--and heaves him off the bow of the speeding ARK--

--ANGLE OFF THE BOW: AHRMAN lands flat on his back, directly in the ARK's path. The juggernaut's shadow falls over him--and a split second later, he is gone, crushed beneath its weight.

NICHOLAS

We must be almost at the bottom of the mountain! We've got to get below deck--! The hull is stronger--thicker wood--!

DR. OLIVER (O.S.)

NICHOLAS--!! LOOK--!!

NICHOLAS and KATRINE turn. Although the ARK is definitely nearing the bottom of the mountain--its SHUDDERING, GRINDING descent is rougher now since the snow and ice are sparser--its speed is still formidable. And up ahead--

NICHOLAS

What's that--?!

KATRINE

(hoarsely)

It looks like...a crowd of people!

There, at the bottom of the mountain, is a MASS of CURIOUS ONLOOKERS. But between these people and the ARK lies an obstacle: a broad, sweeping ramp of rock--and the ARK is barreling straight towards it--

--KATRINE rushes over to PETER, lying on the deck. NICHOLAS joins her. Together, they lift PETER and start half-running up the sloping deck. The ARK rushes towards the rocky ramp--

--DR. OLIVER takes NICHOLAS's BAZOOKA, allowing him to hold PETER more easily. RONIM barks from inside the hatchway. DR. OLIVER risks glancing over his shoulder as he runs--THE ARK HAS ALMOST REACHED THE CURVING SWEEP OF ROCK--

DR. OLIVER

JUMP--! JUMP--!!

He shoves at NICHOLAS and KATRINE and they dive through the hatchway, yanking PETER along with them. DR. OLIVER hurls himself after them, just as the ARK swoops off the rocky ramp

--The ARK sails out into the air, tipping sideways as it goes--

100 - <u>EXT. BOTTOM OF MOUNTAIN - THAT MOMENT</u>

The "GLOBAL BROADCASTING NETWORK" TV film crew has held their position. Although many of the gathered TOWNSPEOPLE have already panicked and run, a substantial CROWD has remained at the bottom of the mountain. On the TV MONITOR, the ARK flies through the air, tipping sideways as it goes, above the words: "LIVE FEED - WORLDWIDE"...

...and now the ARK is coming down, coming down on its side--

CAMERAMAN (V.O.)

Oh...HOLY...SHIT...

More of the ONLOOKERS are running for safety, <u>as the ARK SMASHES back down to earth on its port side</u>. The TV film crew scatters, except for the CAMERAMAN who keeps filming. The ARK slides down the final slope of the mountain, lying on its side, gouging up rocks and stony earth in its path, gradually swinging around as it moves forward. Its speed lessens, its motion impeded by the plowed-up earth and rocks. Eventually, the massive vessel comes to a SHUDDERING halt, entrenched up against the gouged-earth barricade, about sixty feet from the TV VAN. <u>And all at once there is total, overwhelming SILENCE</u>...

The ARK is silent, motionless, lying on its side. No one could have <u>possibly</u> survived this unbelievable mountain descent. And yet, <u>the vessel is still surrounded by a glowing white aura</u>...

Suddenly, a figure lowers from the upended hatchway and drops to the ground. It's KATRINE--<u>uninjured</u>. She walks unsteadily away from the ARK. Then stops, stares about her wonderingly. The TOWNSPEOPLE stare at her the same way. On the TV MONITOR--"LIVE FEED - WORLDWIDE"-- there is a close-up of KATRINE's FACE. She's frowning, puzzled...

KATRINE makes her way down the slope at the bottom of the mountain. She looks as though she is searching for something. IN THE BACKGROUND, DR. OLIVER, RONIM, NICHOLAS and PETER climb down from the ARK. Incredibly, no one seems to have suffered any major injuries.

KATRINE is still frowning, as if listening to something, <u>something calling to only her inside her head</u>. She stops dead in her tracks. She smiles. Slowly, she turns to face the ARK. NICHOLAS and DR. OLIVER are kneeling next to PETER, examining his ankle. KATRINE's gaze rises from them, searching. There! Perched above them on the overturned ARK's hull is <u>the SACRED SENTINEL--the DOVE-- enveloped in a glowing white aura</u>. Suddenly, the sun breaks free of the clouds...

On the TV MONITOR--a <u>CLOSE-UP OF THE DOVE</u>: Its dark eyes are full of benevolent wisdom...the wisdom of the ages. It cocks its head, staring down at KATRINE...

KATRINE gazes joyfully up at the DOVE. Tears flow down her cheeks. The DOVE watches her with its knowing eyes. It is clear that something is about to happen here, something that was <u>meant</u> to happen <u>one thousand years ago</u>...something that is about to happen <u>now</u> because of the powerful pull of DESTINY... A silent communication passes between PRINCESS and HEAVENLY ENTITY. The air SIZZLES between them--<u>and suddenly...finally...it is TIME</u>--

Slowly, KATRINE raises her arms, spreads them wide, her hands opening, palms outward, fingers spread, a gesture of welcome. The DOVE flutters into the air--<u>its body backlit by the sun</u>--and then begins to fly...directly to KATRINE...

...As if IN SLOW MOTION the DOVE flies towards KATRINE. Her arms are still raised, her face tilted to the sky, her eyes closed. The DOVE's wings beat the air, slowly, slowly. We HEAR in our ears, and <u>feel</u> in our hearts, stirring strains of HEAVENLY MUSIC, RISING, RISING. NICHOLAS, DR. OLIVER, PETER and RONIM look on in speechless wonder. As do the gathered TOWNSPEOPLE. As does the still-filming CAMERAMAN--

--And now, we're watching <u>OVER KATRINE'S SHOULDER</u>, as the DOVE approaches, the sun blazing behind it, reducing it to a sharply-defined silhouette: <u>the silhouette of a bird with wings spread joyfully in flight</u>. IN THE IMMEDIATE FOREGROUND: KATRINE's LEFT HAND, raised to the sky--and on the back of her hand is the small odd <u>birthmark</u> that resembles <u>the spread wingspan of a bird in flight</u>. The HEAVENLY MUSIC BECOMES ALL-ENVELOPING. KATRINE, her face tilted to the sky, is bathed in sunlight, arms raised, back arched. And the DOVE swoops directly at KATRINE, not <u>to</u> her--<u>at</u> her--

--As the HEAVENLY MUSIC REACHES A THUNDEROUS CRESCENDO, the swooping DOVE strikes KATRINE dead in the center of her chest--and, as if it has no physical substance whatsoever, <u>continues to fly right through her body</u>--

101 - <u>INT. HOSPITAL ROOM, BARCELONA, SPAIN - MORNING</u>

A TV screen shows the incredible images of <u>the DOVE, flying right through KATRINE's body</u>, above the caption: "GLOBAL BROADCASTING NETWORK (BARCELONA)

NEWS - SPECIAL REPORT - LIVE, VIA SATELLITE, FROM ERTA, TURKEY". A sick, bald YOUNG GIRL watches with bright eyes...

102 - <u>INT. SPORTS BAR, MELBOURNE, AUSTRALIA - EVENING</u>

All customers and employees are breathlessly watching a BIG-SCREEN TV as the SACRED DOVE flies right through KATRINE's body--above the caption: "GLOBAL BROADCASTING NETWORK (MELBOURNE) NEWS - SPECIAL REPORT - LIVE, VIA SATELLITE, FROM ERTA, TURKEY".

103 - <u>INT. BEDROOM, LOS ANGELES, U.S.A. - NIGHT</u>

A TEENAGE BOY about to shoot his arm full of dope is distracted by the television images of the SACRED DOVE flying right through KATRINE's body. The caption on the screen says: "GLOBAL BROADCASTING NETWORK (LOS ANGELES) NEWS - SPECIAL REPORT - LIVE, VIA SATELLITE, FROM ERTA, TURKEY".

104 - <u>EXT. BOTTOM OF MOUNTAIN - THAT MOMENT</u>

--The DOVE <u>soars right through KATRINE</u>, exiting her body between her shoulder-blades. NICHOLAS, DR. OLIVER, PETER and RONIM stare incredulously. The TOWNSPEOPLE gasp and point--and some of them even pray. <u>The CAMERAMAN continues filming</u>. KATRINE's expression is one of absolute peace, total contentment. For a second, <u>we see her enveloped in a glowing white aura</u>. The DOVE's swooping arc takes it back up into the sky...up...up...up...and <u>gone</u>--

NICHOLAS

Katrine?! Katrine...?! Are you all r--?!

He breaks off. For suddenly, an UNEARTHLY SOUND--part-ENRAGED BELLOW, part-TORMENTED SHRIEK--ECHOES down the mountainside. KATRINE's eyes snap open. RONIM SNARLS. The TOWNSPEOPLE turn to stare up the mountain, horrified--

On the mountainside, a shapeless, thrashing SHADOW is gliding towards them at frightening speed. So fast, there's no time to run. As it glides, it continues *to BELLOW/SHRIEK. It comes to a violent stop in front of the ARK. The SHADOW coalesces <u>into the towering figure of the WARLORD AHRMAN</u>. His clothing is in tatters. Rotten patches of white flesh are visible. The holes from NICHOLAS's and DR. OLIVER's BAZOOKA-fire have not healed. Almost all the skin and hair are gone from his face and head; bands of muscle cling to reddened bone. And, still spearing up through his throat, his tongue, his open mouth, up, into his brain, is the STALAGMITE... With that UNEARTHLY SHRIEKING BELLOW ROARING UP from the depths of his decomposing body, AHRMAN's immeasurable fury EXPLODES. He whirls around, flinging his arm outwards, a sweeping BLADE OF GREEN ENERGY shooting from his clenched fist--*

--Like a monstrous SCYTHE, AHRMAN's energy blade slices through the CROWD OF TOWNSPEOPLE, killing MEN, WOMEN, CHILDREN instantly. As the CROWD scatters, KATRINE overcomes her stunned paralysis. She sprints towards AHRMAN.

KATRINE

STOP!! <u>STOP</u>!!!

NICHOLAS is running too, attempting to intercept KATRINE.

NICHOLAS

Katrine, stay back--!!

But she doesn't listen. AHRMAN rounds on her and a FIRE-BALL of ENERGY hurtles from his fist at her. She dives low, avoids the blast, executes a perfect somersault and lands on her feet again. AHRMAN fires another blast, this time at NICHOLAS, running towards him. The blast slams into NICHOLAS's right shoulder and propels him with a CRASH into the hull of the ARK. He lies there, stunned, bleeding. DR. OLIVER hurriedly helps PETER get to a safer place on the other side of the ARK, then returns for NICHOLAS. RONIM barks madly.

AHRMAN swings back to the fleeing TOWNSPEOPLE. ONE, TWO, THREE BLASTS are hurled into the crowd. Bodies go flying--

KATRINE

Stop! STOP!! STOP!!!

KATRINE charges at AHRMAN, leaps on him. She seizes his arm, forces it to one side. His blasts are diverted harmlessly into the ground. He clubs KATRINE aside, kicks her, sends her flying. Meanwhile, NICHOLAS, DR. OLIVER and PETER are desperately trying to re-arm the TWO BAZOOKAS. KATRINE is on her feet, charging at AHRMAN again. Suddenly, the WARLORD begins to levitate, even as he continues to hurl BLAST after BLAST down at the fleeing TOWNSPEOPLE. KATRINE leaps up at him. Her arms encircle his waist--and she is carried up with him into the air--

--ANGLE ON THE TV MONITOR where the images of KATRINE, now rising into the air with AHRMAN, are still being broadcast worldwide--

KATRINE and AHRMAN have risen almost seventy feet before they stop. AHRMAN hammers down on her head and arms, but he can't dislodge her. Below, NICHOLAS and DR. OLIVER are trying to aim their BAZOOKAS at AHRMAN. NICHOLAS, with his scorched and bleeding shoulder, gives up.

NICHOLAS

SHIT--!!
(lowers weapon)
Cornelius, you've got to do this--

DR. OLIVER

But if I hit Katrine--?!
(beat)
And even if I only hit Ahrman--Katrine's not going to stay up there without him!

PETER

You've got to do something! He's gonna push her off him!!

DR. OLIVER takes aim again--and fires. KATRINE, weakening in her struggle with AHRMAN, is given a reprieve as DR. OLIVER's BAZOOKA-fire grazes the side of AHRMAN's rotting face. AHRMAN turns his attention downwards, BLASTING at DR. OLIVER--who dives for cover just in time. Crazed, AHRMAN hurls BLAST after BLAST down at DR. OLIVER, NICHOLAS and PETER sheltering by the ARK. The WARLORD's face and body are visibly, progressively <u>rotting</u>...

With AHRMAN distracted, KATRINE lunges upwards, <u>climbing rapidly up the WARLORD's BODY</u>. She climbs around his torso to his back. Now, it's as if she's piggy-backing with him. She reaches around his neck, grips the end of the STALAGMITE and pulls the long, bloody spike <u>down</u> out of his throat. Then, without hesitation, she <u>plunges it into his chest</u>. AHRMAN's body convulses, then goes very still. For a moment, he and KATRINE just hang there, seventy feet up. Then AHRMAN twists his head around--

AHRMAN

--kill...you...<u>bitch</u>--

The last word SNAPS rotted muscle fibers in AHRMAN's face--<u>his jaw drops open as if he's yawning</u>. The light of dread and panic dawns in his eyes. KATRINE sees what's just happened to his jaw, gets an idea.

KATRINE

(whispers in his ear)
The answer's been right in front of us all the time, hasn't it, you son of a <u>BITCH</u>...

KATRINE lunges higher on his back, reaches over his shoulders and seizes his wrists in an iron grip. AHRMAN struggles, but she is stronger now, <u>her strength clearly a result of her divine experience with the SACRED SENTINEL</u>. She forces his hands together in front of his face, <u>squeezes them into fists</u>. His fists CRACKLE with green energy--and a BLAST shoots <u>harmlessly up into the air</u>. AHRMAN BELLOWS and SHRIEKS. He increases his efforts to unclench his fists, separate his hands, <u>but KATRINE presses and squeezes harder</u>. Another blast fires harmlessly up into the air--

--<u>*ANGLE ON*</u> *NICHOLAS, PETER, DR. OLIVER and RONIM beside the ARK.*

NICHOLAS

It looks...It looks like...she's <u>forcing</u> him to use his sorcery...

PETER

He's gonna rot away to <u>nothing</u>! <u>That's</u> what she's doing! She's gonna make him rot away to <u>nothing</u>!

AHRMAN struggles and thrashes, trying in vain to dislodge KATRINE from his back. BLAST after BLAST of MAGICAL ENERGY shoots from his clamped-together fists, firing harmlessly into the air. Decomposition eats away at him ravenously. BELLOWING, he <u>soars</u> up...up...at least another sixty feet. KATRINE holds on, still forcing him to BLAST harmlessly at empty air. The WARLORD <u>suddenly changes direction</u> and KATRINE's clamped knees lose their grip. AHRMAN dive-bombs towards the rocky earth. But although KATRINE is now <u>only</u> holding on to AHRMAN's wrists, <u>she's still making him BLAST away</u>--

--AHRMAN changes course again, now flying <u>parallel to the ground</u>. He twists--and now KATRINE is between him and the earth. He flies closer and closer to the ground. Her back is torn and shredded by the rocky earth. She screams in agony.

NICHOLAS (O.S.)

Katrine!! Let go!! <u>LET GO</u>!!!

--But KATRINE will <u>not</u> let go. She continues to make AHRMAN BLAST harmlessly up into the air. They're rocketing at the ARK now. DR. OLIVER and NICHOLAS both raise their BAZOOKAS, but there's no time to fire. AHRMAN changes direction yet again, takes them once more <u>up into the sky</u>. He is beyond desperate now. Rotted bits of him are falling off in their rushing wake. He soars up...eighty...ninety... one hundred feet, then abruptly--<u>STOPS</u>. This time, KATRINE's grip is <u>jerked</u> loose completely. Her momentum hurls her up another thirty feet beyond where AHRMAN stopped--

--AHRMAN opens his fists and his BLASTS cease. As KATRINE drops back down, falling past him, the WARLORD grabs the front of her sweater in his rotting hand. He lifts her so that their faces are level. His lower jaw dangles from only one side of his face. His visible flesh is erupting with still more decaying lesions. But still he raises his rotting fist, draws it back to deliver a killing blow--

--Suddenly, AHRMAN's body convulses--convulses--and convulses again. In his face: shock, terror. He gags, retches, and COUGHS. We HEAR some part of his insides...RUPTURE. And then he starts to vomit--a spewing cascade of SQUIRMING YELLOW MAGGOTS. The convulsing and vomiting continue for almost ten seconds--then suddenly his head snaps back and, with emphatic finality, the life vanishes from his eyes--

--KATRINE's sweater is released--and she starts to fall--

NICHOLAS (O.S.)

KATRINE--!!!

--Instinctively, KATRINE grabs hold of AHRMAN's CORPSE and together they plummet. NICHOLAS, DR. OLIVER and RONIM run out into the open, with no way to prevent the inevitable. KATRINE clutches AHRMAN's body tightly--and just before they hit the ground, she twists around in mid-air so that AHRMAN's CORPSE is below her and--WHAM!--they come to earth--

--AHRMAN's BODY hits first and KATRINE is thrown violently off to one side. The WARLORD's torso has burst open. Churning masses of MAGGOTS spill out. There is a momentary CRACKLE of MAGICAL ENERGY that SIZZLES through the CORPSE, then FIZZLES out completely...gone--

KATRINE lies as still as death. NICHOLAS falls to his knees next to her. DR. OLIVER, supporting PETER, and RONIM hurry over as well. NICHOLAS reaches out to touch KATRINE's pale face--and suddenly, she stirs, opens her eyes! And just for a second, we see her enveloped in a glowing white aura... KATRINE *pushes herself up, trying unsteadily to get to her feet. NICHOLAS places his hand on her shoulder.*

NICHOLAS

Wait... <u>Wait</u>--

But she won't wait. She struggles to her feet.

NICHOLAS

(standing)
Katrine--what's--?

KATRINE

Have to see...! Have to <u>see</u>--!

KATRINE pushes past NICHOLAS and stumbles over to AHRMAN'S BODY. The CORPSE literally disintegrates before our eyes, turning to dust that swirls away on the wind. The MAGGOTS burrow into the earth. All that is left of the WARLORD AHRMAN is a <u>skeleton</u>. And that, too, turns rapidly to dust. Until finally only one last thing remains: <u>AHRMAN's SKULL</u>--

--<u>CRUNCH</u>!--Suddenly, KATRINE's BOOT comes down <u>INTO FRAME</u>, smashing AHRMAN's SKULL into pieces--<u>CRUNCH</u>!--into fragments--<u>CRUNCH</u>! <u>CRUNCH</u>! <u>CRUNCH</u>!--into tiny bits, into <u>powder</u>... There are tears streaming down KATRINE's cheeks as her boot continues to GRIND and GRIND. And NICHOLAS is standing beside her, his eyes also filled with tears; and behind him is DR. OLIVER, with PETER holding on to his arm for support; and RONIM--

AND OFF TO ONE SIDE: THE CAMERAMAN, filming, filming...

The gray dust that was AHRMAN disperses in the wind. KATRINE is openly weeping.

KATRINE

He's...finished...Father. He's finished... He's...<u>gone</u>--

FATALISM

She stumbles away...into NICHOLAS's arms...

FADE TO:

<u>*TOTAL BLACKNESS*</u>. *The descending ENGINE-NOISE of an AIRPLANE coming in for a landing. A CAPTION appears:* **NORTHERN EUROPE ~ AD 2005**.

DISSOLVE TO:

105 - <u>INT. MINI-VAN - MOVING - MORNING</u>

NICHOLAS is driving, with KATRINE beside him. PETER is behind them and, at the very back of the vehicle, sit DR. OLIVER and his wife, holding hands. RONIM lies comfortably between them, his chin in DR. OLIVER's lap. Everyone looks rested and healthy--<u>but KATRINE is also nervous</u>. In her lap is a newspaper, with a July date--about two months have passed since the climactic events in Turkey.

<u>*CLOSE-UP*</u> *ON THE NEWSPAPER's MAIN HEADLINE:* **NOAH'S ARK AUTHENTICATED**. *Below that, a secondary headline:* **UNITED NATIONS OFFERS 'PRINCESS FROM THE PAST' POSITION AS HONORARY WORLD AMBASSADOR OF PEACE**. *Below this headline is a STILL-PHOTOGRAPH taken from the "GLOBAL BROADCASTING NETWORK" footage of the events that occurred at the bottom of the mountain: KATRINE standing with her arms raised, frozen at the moment that the SACRED DOVE was passing through her body...*

KATRINE is looking anxiously through the mini-van's windows. The vehicle goes around a curve in the road. <u>Suddenly, KATRINE GASPS</u>. She sits forward, her eyes widening, her face turning pale.

<u>*KATRINE's POV*</u>: *In the distance are a few acres of park-land--and the ancient, crumbled ruins of <u>KING GALEN's CASTLE</u>...*

DISSOLVE TO:

106 - <u>EXT. CASTLE RUINS - AFTERNOON</u>

NICHOLAS is sitting alone on a pile of rubble. KATRINE drifts slowly through the ruins, overwhelmed, her cheeks wet. At her side, RONIM is sniffing ancient ghosts. KATRINE and RONIM, home again after <u>ten long centuries</u>...

NICHOLAS goes to KATRINE, links his arm with hers.

NICHOLAS

How are you doing?

KATRINE

(trying to smile)
They're all here, Nicholas. I can feel them, hear them. My father, my mother, Marcus, Firebrand. <u>Alexander</u>.

NICHOLAS doesn't know what to say. After a tactful pause:

NICHOLAS

Shall we...umm...maybe we should go...join the others...?

KATRINE looks at him, tears sparkling in her eyes.

KATRINE

There's just one more thing...one more thing I have to see...
(pause)
One more thing I need to know...

107 - <u>EXT. BANK OF A STREAM - AFTERNOON</u>

KATRINE and NICHOLAS are sitting on the bank of a stream. The CASTLE RUINS are visible in the background. RONIM is lying beneath an ancient oak tree. KATRINE is removing her boots and socks while NICHOLAS watches, mystified.

FATALISM

KATRINE

(emotions taut)

This tree...was little more than a sapling the last time I saw it...

NICHOLAS

But...why have we come here...?

KATRINE jumps to her feet. NICHOLAS follows as she hurries to the water's edge.

KATRINE

When Alexander and I were children, we found a place...down here...by the riverbank--
(pause)
There--

KATRINE points at a JUTTING SLAB OF ROCK, extending from the bank about two feet, just below the surface of the water. Then, still wearing jeans and a shirt, she steps quickly <u>into the stream</u>--

NICHOLAS

What are you <u>doing</u>?! You can't! <u>KATRINE</u>--!

KATRINE turns back to him, her eyes very bright.

KATRINE

It's our secret place, Nicholas. Our secret hiding place...

Before he can say anything, KATRINE wades further out. And there, where the JUTTING SLAB OF ROCK comes to an end, she carefully <u>sits down</u>, takes a deep breath--and then <u>lies back, face up, in the water</u>, completely submerging herself, head and all--

NICHOLAS

<u>Katrine</u>--!!

155

--Finally, just visible beneath the surface, <u>she begins to disappear under the ROCK SLAB</u>--

108 - <u>EXT. UNDER THE STREAM'S SURFACE - THAT MOMENT</u>

Lying flat on her back, KATRINE <u>pulls herself</u> along under the water, using finger-holds on the underside of the ROCK SLAB. She's moving <u>in towards the bank</u>.

<u>FLASHBACK (in her mind)</u>: ALEXANDER, riding on horseback out of the secret tunnel exit, his long hair wet and slicked back--

                          KATRINE
Where did you get to? And why are you all wet--?

                         ALEXANDER
There was something I had to do...

<u>FLASHBACK (in her mind)</u>: ALEXANDER, talking to MARCUS at her bedroom doorway--

                         ALEXANDER
(voice lowered)
I've been planning this for months...

KATRINE breaks the water's surface. She has come up in a tiny cave scooped out under the rocky riverbank. One of her hands reaches up the wall, finds a natural rock ledge well above the water-line. Her fingers close around something--an <u>EARTHENWARE CANISTER</u>...

109 - <u>EXT. BANK OF A STREAM - AFTERNOON</u>

KATRINE, NICHOLAS and RONIM are back up on the bank. They're all wet, but KATRINE is soaked, shivering, with NICHOLAS's jacket around her shoulders. She turns the CANISTER slowly over in her hands.

KATRINE

Could he ever have imagined that it would stay where he hid it--<u>for one thousand years</u>...?

She looks at NICHOLAS, her eyes gleaming. Then, drawing a deep breath, she twists off the CANISTER's air-tight lid. With trembling fingers, she pulls out: <u>AN EXQUISITE GOLD RING</u>...

KATRINE stares at the RING lying in her palm for a long, long moment. Then her trembling hand closes into a fist and presses, presses against her breast. We see the birthmark on the back of her hand, the birthmark in the shape of the spread wingspan of a bird in flight. Overcome with grief and loss, she begins to shake. NICHOLAS takes her in his arms and holds on very, very tightly...

...AND <u>OUR POV</u> PULLS BACK...BACK...ANGLING SLOWLY AROUND AS WE SWING UP...UP...away from them. They diminish in OUR VIEW, becoming smaller and smaller, still holding on to each other, smaller, smaller, as we move back and back...

...<u>OUR POV</u> pulls all the way back to the ruins of KING GALEN's CASTLE, so that we're now looking at the THREE SMALL FIGURES--KATRINE, NICHOLAS and RONIM-- from the vantage point of one of the crumbled battlements...where, perched right in front of us, gazing in the same direction, is a DOVE--<u>a beautiful white DOVE</u>...

...Suddenly, the DOVE's wings open...flutter...and it takes off into the sky...

<u>OUR POV</u> follows it...up...up...and eventually it disappears, as its pure whiteness blends with the blinding brilliance of the sun...

...a blinding brilliance that suffuses the ENTIRE FRAME...as we...

FADE OUT.